Reginald's Christmas Revel

Saki

Reginald's
Christmas Revel

PENGUIN CLASSICS
an imprint of
PENGUIN BOOKS

PENGUIN CLASSICS

UK | USA | Canada | Ireland | Australia
India | New Zealand | South Africa

Penguin Books is part of the Penguin Random House group of companies
whose addresses can be found at global.penguinrandomhouse.com.

Stories first published between 1904 and 1919
This selection taken from *The Complete Short Stories*, Penguin Classics, 2000
This edition published in Little Clothbound Classics 2022
001

Cover design and illustration by Coralie Bickford-Smith

Set in 9.5/13pt Baskerville 10 Pro
Typeset by Jouve (UK), Milton Keynes
Printed and bound in Great Britain by Clays Ltd, Elcograf S.p.A.

The authorized representative in the EEA is Penguin Random House Ireland,
Morrison Chambers, 32 Nassau Street, Dublin D02 YH68

A CIP catalogue record for this book is available from the British Library

ISBN: 978-0-241-59702-6

www.greenpenguin.co.uk

Contents

Contents

Reginald's Christmas Revel

They say (said Reginald) that there's nothing sadder than victory except defeat. If you've ever stayed with dull people during what is alleged to be the festive season, you can probably revise that saying. I shall never forget putting in a Christmas at the Babwolds'. Mrs Babwold is some relation of my father's – a sort of to-be-left-till-called-for cousin – and that was considered sufficient reason for my having to accept her invitation at about the sixth time of asking; though why the sins of the father should be visited by the children – you won't find any notepaper in that drawer; that's where I keep old menus and first-night programmes.

Mrs Babwold wears a rather solemn personality, and has never been known to smile, even when saying disagreeable things to her friends or making out the Stores list. She takes her pleasures sadly. A state elephant at a Durbar gives one a very similar impression. Her husband gardens in all weathers. When a man goes out in the pouring rain to brush caterpillars off rose trees, I generally imagine his life indoors leaves something to be desired; anyway, it must be very unsettling for the caterpillars.

Of course there were other people there. There was a Major Somebody who had shot things in Lapland, or somewhere of that sort; I forget what they were, but it wasn't for want of reminding. We had them cold with every meal almost, and he was continually giving us details of what they measured from tip to tip, as though he thought we were going to make them warm underthings for the winter. I used to listen to him with a rapt attention that I thought rather suited me, and then one day I quite modestly gave the dimensions of an okapi I had shot in the Lincolnshire fens. The Major turned a beautiful Tyrian scarlet (I remember thinking at the time that I should like my bathroom hung in that colour), and I think that at that moment he almost found it in his heart to dislike me. Mrs Babwold put on a first-aid-to-the-injured expression, and asked him why he didn't publish a book of his sporting reminiscences; it would be *so* interesting. She didn't remember till afterwards that he had given her two fat volumes on the subject, with his portrait and autograph as a frontispiece and an appendix on the habits of the Arctic mussel.

It was in the evening that we cast aside the cares and distractions of the day and really lived. Cards were thought to be too frivolous and empty a way of passing the time, so most of them played what they called a book game. You went out into the hall – to get an inspiration, I suppose – then you came in again with a muffler tied round your neck and looked silly, and the others were supposed to guess that you were *Wee MacGreegor*. I held out against the inanity as long as I decently could, but at last, in a lapse of good nature, I consented to masquerade as a book, only I warned them that it would take some time to carry out. They waited for the best part of forty minutes while I went and played wineglass skittles with the page-boy in the pantry; you play it with a champagne cork, you know, and the one who knocks down the most glasses without breaking them wins. I won, with four unbroken out of seven; I think William suffered from over-anxiousness. They were rather mad in the drawing-room at my not having come back, and they weren't a bit pacified when I told them afterwards that I was *At the end of the passage*.

'I never did like Kipling,' was Mrs Babwold's comment, when the situation dawned upon her. 'I couldn't see anything clever in *Earthworms out of Tuscany – or* is that by Darwin?'

Of course these games are very educational, but, personally, I prefer bridge.

On Christmas evening we were supposed to be specially festive in the Old English fashion. The hall was horribly draughty, but it seemed to be the proper place to revel in, and it was decorated with Japanese fans and Chinese lanterns, which gave it a very Old English effect.

Saki

A young lady with a confidential voice favoured us with a long recitation about a little girl who died or did something equally hackneyed, and then the Major gave us a graphic account of a struggle he had with a wounded bear. I privately wished that the bears would win sometimes on these occasions; at least they wouldn't go vapouring about it afterwards. Before we had time to recover our spirits, we were indulged with some thought-reading by a young man whom one knew instinctively had a good mother and an indifferent tailor – the sort of young man who talks unflaggingly through the thickest soup, and smooths his hair dubiously as though he thought it might hit back. The thought-reading was rather a success; he announced that the hostess was thinking about poetry, and she admitted that her mind was dwelling on one of Austin's odes. Which was near enough. I fancy she had been really wondering whether a scrag-end of mutton and some cold plum-pudding would do for the kitchen dinner next day. As a crowning dissipation, they all sat down to play progressive halma, with milk-chocolate for prizes. I've been carefully brought up, and I don't like to play games of skill for milk-chocolate, so I invented a headache and retired from the scene. I had been preceded a few minutes earlier by Miss Langshan-Smith, a rather formidable lady, who always got up at some uncomfortable hour in the morning, and gave you the impression that she had been in communication with most of the European Governments before breakfast. There was a paper pinned on her door with a signed request that she might be called particularly early on the morrow. Such an opportunity does not come twice in a lifetime. I covered up everything except the signature with another notice, to the effect that before these words should meet the eye she would have ended a misspent life, was sorry for the trouble she was giving, and would like a military funeral. A few minutes later I violently exploded an air-filled paper bag on the landing, and gave a stage moan that could have been heard in the cellars. Then I pursued my original intention and went to bed. The noise those people made in forcing open the good lady's door was positively indecorous; she resisted gallantly, but I believe they searched her for bullets for about a quarter of an hour, as if she had been a historic battlefield.

I hate travelling on Boxing Day, but one must occasionally do things that one dislikes.

Reginald's Choir Treat

'Never,' wrote Reginald to his most darling friend, 'be a pioneer. It's the Early Christian that gets the fattest lion.'

Reginald, in his way, was a pioneer.

None of the rest of his family had anything approaching Titian hair or a sense of humour, and they used primroses as a table decoration.

It follows that they never understood Reginald, who came down late to breakfast, and nibbled toast, and said disrespectful things about the universe. The family ate porridge, and believed in everything, even the weather forecast.

Therefore the family was relieved when the vicar's daughter undertook the reformation of Reginald. Her name was Amabel; it was the vicar's one extravagance. Amabel was accounted a beauty and intellectually gifted; she never played tennis, and was reputed to have read Maeterlinck's *Life of the Bee*. If you abstain from tennis *and* read Maeterlinck in a small country village, you are of necessity intellectual. Also she had been twice to

Fécamp to pick up a good French accent from the Americans staying there; consequently she had a knowledge of the world which might be considered useful in dealings with a worldling.

Hence the congratulations in the family when Amabel undertook the reformation of its wayward member.

Amabel commenced operations by asking her unsuspecting pupil to tea in the vicarage garden; she believed in the healthy influence of natural surroundings, never having been in Sicily, where things are different.

And like every woman who has ever preached repentance to unregenerate youth, she dwelt on the sin of an empty life, which always seems so much more scandalous in the country, where people rise early to see if a new strawberry has happened during the night.

Reginald recalled the lilies of the field, 'which simply sat and looked beautiful, and defied competition'.

'But that is not an example for us to follow,' gasped Amabel.

'Unfortunately, we can't afford to. You don't know what a world of trouble I take in trying to rival the lilies in their artistic simplicity.'

'You are really indecently vain of your appearance. A good life is infinitely preferable to good looks.'

'You agree with me that the two are incompatible. I always say beauty is only sin deep.'

Amabel began to realize that the battle is not always to the strong-minded. With the immemorial resource of

7

her sex, she abandoned the frontal attack and laid stress on her unassisted labours in parish work, her mental loneliness, her discouragements – and at the right moment she produced strawberries and cream. Reginald was obviously affected by the latter, and when his preceptress suggested that he might begin the strenuous life by helping her to supervise the annual outing of the bucolic infants who composed the local choir, his eyes shone with the dangerous enthusiasm of a convert.

Reginald entered on the strenuous life alone, as far as Amabel was concerned. The most virtuous women are not proof against damp grass, and Amabel kept her bed with a cold. Reginald called it a dispensation; it had been the dream of his life to stage-manage a choir outing. With strategic insight, he led his shy, bullet-headed charges to the nearest woodland stream and allowed them to bathe; then he seated himself on their discarded garments and discoursed on their immediate future, which, he decreed, was to embrace a Bacchanalian procession through the village. Forethought had provided the occasion with a supply of tin whistles, but the introduction of a he-goat from a neighbouring orchard was a brilliant afterthought. Properly, Reginald explained, there should have been an outfit of panther skins; as it was, those who had spotted handkerchiefs were allowed to wear them, which they did with thankfulness. Reginald recognized the impossibility, in the time at his disposal, of teaching his shivering neophytes a chant in honour of Bacchus, so he started them off with a more familiar, if less appropriate, temperance hymn. After all, he said, it is the spirit of the thing that counts. Following the etiquette of dramatic authors on first nights, he remained discreetly in the background while the procession, with extreme diffidence and the goat, wound its way lugubriously towards the village. The singing had died down long before the main street was reached, but the miserable wailing of pipes brought the inhabitants to their doors. Reginald said he had seen something like it in pictures; the villagers had seen nothing like it in their lives, and remarked as much freely.

Reginald's family never forgave him. They had no sense of humour.

Reginald on Christmas Presents

I wish it to be distinctly understood (said Reginald) that I don't want a 'George, Prince of Wales' Prayer-book as a Christmas present. The fact cannot be too widely known.

There ought (he continued) to be technical education classes on the science of present-giving. No one seems to have the faintest notion of what anyone else wants, and the prevalent ideas on the subject are not creditable to a civilized community.

There is, for instance, the female relative in the country who 'knows a tie is always useful', and sends you some spotted horror that you could only wear in secret or in Tottenham Court Road. It *might* have been useful had she kept it to tie up currant bushes with, when it would have served the double purpose of supporting the branches and frightening away the birds – for it is an admitted fact that the ordinary tomtit of commerce has a sounder aesthetic taste than the average female relative in the country.

Then there are aunts. They are always a difficult class to

deal with in the matter of presents. The trouble is that one never catches them really young enough. By the time one has educated them to an appreciation of the fact that one does not wear red woollen mittens in the West End, they die, or quarrel with the family, or do something equally inconsiderate. That is why the supply of trained aunts is always so precarious.

There is my Aunt Agatha, *par exemple*, who sent me a pair of gloves last Christmas, and even got so far as to choose a kind that was being worn and had the correct number of buttons. But – *they were nines!* I sent them to a boy whom I hated intimately: he didn't wear them, of course, but he could have – that was where the bitterness of death came in. It was nearly as consoling as sending white flowers to his funeral. Of course I wrote and told my aunt that they were the one thing that had been wanting to make existence blossom like a rose; I am afraid she thought me frivolous – she comes from the North, where they live in the fear of Heaven and the Earl of Durham. (Reginald affects an exhaustive knowledge of things political, which furnishes an excellent excuse for not discussing them.) Aunts with a dash of foreign extraction in them are the most satisfactory in the way of understanding these things; but if you can't choose your aunt, it is wisest in the long run to choose the present and send her the bill.

Even friends of one's own set, who might be expected to know better, have curious delusions on the subject. I am *not* collecting copies of the cheaper editions of Omar

Khayyám. I gave the last four that I received to the lift-boy, and I like to think of him reading them, with FitzGerald's notes, to his aged mother. Lift-boys always have aged mothers; shows such nice feeling on their part, I think.

Personally, I can't see where the difficulty in choosing suitable presents lies. No boy who had brought himself up properly could fail to appreciate one of those decorative bottles of liqueurs that are so reverently staged in Morel's window – and it wouldn't in the least matter if one did get duplicates. And there would always be the supreme moment of dreadful uncertainty whether it was *crème de menthe* or Chartreuse – like the expectant thrill on seeing your part-ner's hand turned up at bridge. People may say what they like about the decay of Christianity; the religious system that produced green Chartreuse can never really die.

And then, of course, there are liqueur glasses, and crys-tallized fruits, and tapestry curtains, and heaps of other necessaries of life that make really sensible presents – not to speak of luxuries, such as having one's bills paid, or getting something quite sweet in the way of jewellery. Unlike the alleged Good Woman of the Bible, I'm not above rubies. When found, by the way, she must have been rather a problem at Christmas-time; nothing short of a blank cheque would have fitted the situation. Perhaps it's as well that she's died out.

The great charm about me (concluded Reginald) is that I am so easily pleased. But I draw the line at a 'Prince of Wales' Prayer-book.

The Reticence of Lady Anne

Egbert came into the large, dimly lit drawing-room with the air of a man who is not certain whether he is entering a dovecote or a bomb factory, and is prepared for either eventuality. The little domestic quarrel over the luncheon-table had not been fought to a definite finish, and the question was how far Lady Anne was in a mood to renew or forgo hostilities. Her pose in the arm-chair by the tea-table was rather elaborately rigid; in the gloom of a December afternoon Egbert's pince-nez did not materially help him to discern the expression of her face.

By way of breaking whatever ice might be floating on the surface he made a remark about a dim religious light. He or Lady Anne were accustomed to make that remark between 4.30 and 6 on winter and late autumn evenings; it was a part of their married life. There was no recognized rejoinder to it, and Lady Anne made none.

Don Tarquinio lay astretch on the Persian rug, basking in the firelight with superb indifference to the possible ill-humour of Lady Anne. His pedigree was as flawlessly

Persian as the rug, and his ruff was coming into the glory of its second winter. The page-boy, who had Renaissance tendencies, had christened him Don Tarquinio. Left to themselves, Egbert and Lady Anne would unfailingly have called him Fluff, but they were not obstinate.

Egbert poured himself out some tea. As the silence gave no sign of breaking on Lady Anne's initiative, he braced himself for another Yermak effort.

'My remark at lunch had a purely academic application,' he announced; 'you seem to put an unnecessarily personal significance into it.'

Lady Anne maintained her defensive barrier of silence. The bullfinch lazily filled in the interval with an air from *Iphigénie en Tauride.* Egbert recognized it immediately, because it was the only air the bullfinch whistled, and he had come to them with the reputation for whistling it. Both Egbert and Lady Anne would have preferred something from *The Yeoman of the Guard,* which was their favourite opera. In matters artistic they had a similarity of taste. They leaned towards the honest and explicit in art, a picture, for instance, that told its own story, with generous assistance from its title. A riderless warhorse with harness in obvious disarray, staggering into a courtyard full of pale swooning women, and marginally noted 'Bad News,' suggested to their minds a distinct interpretation of some military catastrophe. They could see what it was meant to convey, and explain it to friends of duller intelligence.

The silence continued. As a rule Lady Anne's displeasure became articulate and markedly voluble after four minutes of introductory muteness. Egbert seized the milk-jug and poured some of its contents into Don Tarquinio's saucer; as the saucer was already full to the brim an unsightly overflow was the result. Don Tarquinio looked on with a surprised interest that evanesced into elaborate unconsciousness when he was appealed to by Egbert to come and drink up some of the spilt matter. Don Tarquinio was prepared to play many rôles in life, but a vacuum carpet-cleaner was not one of them.

'Don't you think we're being rather foolish?' said Egbert cheerfully.

If Lady Anne thought so she didn't say so.

'I daresay the fault has been partly on my side,' continued Egbert, with evaporating cheerfulness. 'After all, I'm only human, you know. You seem to forget that I'm only human.'

He insisted on the point, as if there had been unfounded suggestions that he was built on Satyr lines, with goat continuations where the human left off.

The bullfinch recommenced its air from *Iphigénie en Tauride*. Egbert began to feel depressed. Lady Anne was not drinking her tea. Perhaps she was feeling unwell. But when Lady Anne felt unwell she was not wont to be reticent on the subject. 'No one knows what I suffer from indigestion' was one of her favourite statements; but the lack of knowledge can only have been caused by defective listening; the amount of information available on the subject would have supplied material for a monograph.

Evidently Lady Anne was not feeling unwell.

Egbert began to think he was being unreasonably dealt with; naturally he began to make concessions.

'I daresay,' he observed, taking as central a position on the hearth-rug as Don Tarquinio could be persuaded to concede him, 'I may have been to blame. I am willing, if I can thereby restore things to a happier standpoint, to undertake to lead a better life.'

He wondered vaguely how it would be possible. Temptations came to him, in middle age, tentatively and without insistence, like a neglected butcher-boy who asks for a Christmas box in February for no more hopeful reason than that he didn't get one in December. He had no more idea of succumbing to them than he had of purchasing the fish-knives and fur boas that ladies are impelled to sacrifice through the medium of advertisement columns during twelve months of the year. Still, there was something impressive in this unasked-for renunciation of possibly latent enormities.

Lady Anne showed no sign of being impressed.

Egbert looked at her nervously through his glasses. To get the worst of an argument with her was no new experience. To get the worst of a monologue was a humiliating novelty.

'I shall go and dress for dinner,' he announced in a

voice into which he intended some shade of sternness to creep.

At the door a final access of weakness impelled him to make a further appeal.

'Aren't we being very silly?'

'A fool,' was Don Tarquinio's mental comment as the door closed on Egbert's retreat. Then he lifted his velvet forepaws in the air and leapt lightly on to a bookshelf immediately under the bullfinch's cage. It was the first time he had seemed to notice the bird's existence, but he was carrying out a long-formed theory of action with the precision of mature deliberation. The bullfinch, who had fancied himself something of a despot, depressed himself of a sudden into a third of his normal displacement; then he fell to a helpless wing-beating and shrill cheeping. He had cost twenty-seven shillings without the cage, but Lady Anne made no sign of interfering. She had been dead for two hours.

Gabriel-Ernest

'There is a wild beast in your woods,' said the artist Cunningham, as he was being driven to the station. It was the only remark he had made during the drive, but as Van Cheele had talked incessantly his companion's silence had not been noticeable.

'A stray fox or two and some resident weasels. Nothing more formidable,' said Van Cheele. The artist said nothing.

'What did you mean about a wild beast?' said Van Cheele later, when they were on the platform.

'Nothing. My imagination. Here is the train,' said Cunningham.

That afternoon Van Cheele went for one of his frequent rambles through his woodland property. He had a stuffed bittern in his study, and knew the names of quite a number of wild flowers, so his aunt had possibly some justification in describing him as a great naturalist. At any rate, he was a great walker. It was his custom to take mental notes of everything he saw during his walks, not so much for the purpose of assisting contemporary science as to provide topics for conversation afterwards. When the bluebells began to show themselves in flower he made a point of informing every one of the fact; the season of the year might have warned his hearers of the likelihood of such an occurrence, but at least they felt that he was being absolutely frank with them.

What Van Cheele saw on this particular afternoon was, however, something far removed from his ordinary range of experience. On a shelf of smooth stone overhanging a deep pool in the hollow of an oak coppice a boy of about sixteen lay asprawl, drying his wet brown limbs luxuriously in the sun. His wet hair, parted by a recent dive, lay close to his head, and his light-brown eyes, so light that there was an almost tigerish gleam in them, were turned towards Van Cheele with a certain lazy watchfulness. It was an unexpected apparition, and Van Cheele found himself engaged in the novel process of thinking before he spoke. Where on earth could this wild-looking boy hail from? The miller's wife had lost a child some two months ago, supposed to have been swept away by the millrace, but that had been a mere baby, not a half-grown lad.

'What are you doing there?' he demanded.

'Obviously, sunning myself,' replied the boy.

'Where do you live?'

'Here, in these woods.'

'You can't live in the woods,' said Van Cheele.

'They are very nice woods,' said the boy, with a touch of patronage in his voice.

'But where do you sleep at night?'

'I don't sleep at night; that's my busiest time.'

Van Cheele began to have an irritated feeling that he was grappling with a problem that was eluding him.

'What do you feed on?' he asked.

'Flesh,' said the boy, and he pronounced the word with slow relish, as though he were tasting it.

'Flesh! What flesh?'

'Since it interests you, rabbits, wild-fowl, hares, poultry, lambs in their season, children when I can get any; they're usually too well locked in at night, when I do most of my hunting. It's quite two months since I tasted child-flesh.'

Ignoring the chaffing nature of the last remark Van Cheele tried to draw the boy on the subject of possible poaching operations.

'You're talking rather through your hat when you speak of feeding on hares.' (Considering the nature of the boy's toilet the simile was hardly an apt one.) 'Our hillside hares aren't easily caught.'

'At night I hunt on four feet,' was the somewhat cryptic response.

'I suppose you mean that you hunt with a dog?' hazarded Van Cheele.

The boy rolled slowly over on to his back, and laughed

a weird low laugh, that was pleasantly like a chuckle and disagreeably like a snarl.

'I don't fancy any dog would be very anxious for my company, especially at night.'

Van Cheele began to feel that there was something positively uncanny about the strange-eyed, strange-tongued youngster.

'I can't have you staying in these woods,' he declared authoritatively.

'I fancy you'd rather have me here than in your house,' said the boy.

The prospect of this wild, nude animal in Van Cheele's primly ordered house was certainly an alarming one.

'If you don't go I shall have to make you,' said Van Cheele.

The boy turned like a flash, plunged into the pool, and in a moment had flung his wet and glistening body half-way up the bank where Van Cheele was standing. In an otter the movement would not have been remarkable; in a boy Van Cheele found it sufficiently startling. His foot slipped as he made an involuntary backward movement, and he found himself almost prostrate on the slippery weed-grown bank, with those tigerish yellow eyes not very far from his own. Almost instinctively he half raised his hand to his throat. The boy laughed again, a laugh in which the snarl had nearly driven out the chuckle, and then, with another of his astonishing lightning movements, plunged out of view into a yielding tangle of weed and fern.

'What an extraordinary wild animal!' said Van Cheele as he picked himself up. And then he recalled Cunningham's remark, 'There is a wild beast in your woods.'

Walking slowly homeward, Van Cheele began to turn over in his mind various local occurrences which might be traceable to the existence of this astonishing young savage.

Something had been thinning the game in the woods lately, poultry had been missing from the farms, hares were growing unaccountably scarcer, and complaints had reached him of lambs being carried off bodily from the hills. Was it possible that this wild boy was really hunting the countryside in company with some clever poacher dog? He had spoken of hunting 'four-footed' by night, but then, again, he had hinted strangely at no dog caring to come near him, 'especially at night.' It was certainly puzzling. And then, as Van Cheele ran his mind over the various depredations that had been committed during the last month or two, he came suddenly to a dead stop, alike in his walk and his speculations. The child missing from the mill two months ago – the accepted theory was that it had tumbled into the mill-race and been swept away; but the mother had always declared she had heard a shriek on the hill side of the house, in the opposite direction from the water. It was unthinkable, of course, but he wished that the boy had not made that uncanny remark about childflesh eaten two months ago. Such dreadful things should not be said even in fun.

Van Cheele, contrary to his usual wont, did not feel disposed to be communicative about his discovery in the wood. His position as a parish councillor and justice of the peace seemed somehow compromised by the fact that he was harbouring a personality of such doubtful repute on his property; there was even a possibility that a heavy bill of damages for raided lambs and poultry might be laid at his door. At dinner that night he was quite unusually silent.

'Where's your voice gone to?' said his aunt. 'One would think you had seen a wolf.'

Van Cheele, who was not familiar with the old saying, thought the remark rather foolish; if he *had* seen a wolf on his property his tongue would have been extraordinarily busy with the subject.

At breakfast next morning Van Cheele was conscious that his feeling of uneasiness regarding yesterday's episode had not wholly disappeared, and he resolved to go by train to the neighbouring cathedral town, hunt up Cunningham, and learn from him what he had really seen that had prompted the remark about a wild beast in the woods. With this resolution taken, his usual cheerfulness partially returned, and he hummed a bright little melody as he sauntered to the morning-room for his customary cigarette. As he entered the room the melody made way abruptly for a pious invocation. Gracefully asprawl on the ottoman, in an attitude of almost exaggerated repose, was the boy of the woods. He was drier than when Van Cheele had last seen him, but no other alteration was noticeable in his toilet.

'How dare you come here?' asked Van Cheele furiously.

'You told me I was not to stay in the woods,' said the boy calmly.

'But not to come here. Supposing my aunt should see you!'

And with a view to minimizing that catastrophe Van Cheele hastily obscured as much of his unwelcome guest as possible under the folds of a *Morning Post*. At that moment his aunt entered the room.

'This is a poor boy who has lost his way – and lost his memory. He doesn't know who he is or where he comes from,' explained Van Cheele desperately, glancing apprehensively at the waif's face to see whether he was going to add inconvenient candour to his other savage propensities.

Miss Van Cheele was enormously interested.

'Perhaps his underlinen is marked,' she suggested.

'He seems to have lost most of that, too,' said Van Cheele, making frantic little grabs at the *Morning Post* to keep it in its place.

A naked homeless child appealed to Miss Van Cheele as warmly as a stray kitten or derelict puppy would have done.

'We must do all we can for him,' she decided, and in a very short time a messenger, dispatched to the rectory, where a page-boy was kept, had returned with a suit of pantry clothes, and the necessary accessories of shirt, shoes, collar, etc. Clothed, clean, and groomed, the boy lost none of his uncanniness in Van Cheele's eyes, but his aunt found him sweet.

'We must call him something till we know who he really is,' she said. 'Gabriel-Ernest, I think; those are nice suitable names.'

Van Cheele agreed, but he privately doubted whether they were being grafted on to a nice suitable child. His misgivings were not diminished by the fact that his staid and elderly spaniel had bolted out of the house at the first incoming of the boy, and now obstinately remained shivering and yapping at the farther end of the orchard, while the canary, usually as vocally industrious as Van Cheele himself, had put itself on an allowance of frightened cheeps. More than ever he was resolved to consult Cunningham without loss of time.

As he drove off to the station his aunt was arranging that Gabriel-Ernest should help her to entertain the infant members of her Sunday-school class at tea that afternoon.

Cunningham was not at first disposed to be communicative.

'My mother died of some brain trouble,' he explained, 'so you will understand why I am averse to dwelling on anything of an impossibly fantastic nature that I may see or think that I have seen.'

'But what *did* you see?' persisted Van Cheele.

'What I thought I saw was something so extraordinary that no really sane man could dignify it with the credit of having actually happened. I was standing, the last evening I was with you, half-hidden in the hedgegrowth by the orchard gate, watching the dying glow of the sunset. Suddenly I became aware of a naked boy, a bather from some neighbouring pool, I took him to be, who was standing out on the bare hillside also watching the sunset. His pose was so suggestive of some wild faun of Pagan myth that I instantly wanted to engage him as a model, and in another moment I think I should have hailed him. But just then the sun dipped out of view, and all the orange and pink slid out of the landscape, leaving it cold and grey. And at the same moment an astounding thing happened – the boy vanished too!'

'What! vanished away into nothing?' asked Van Cheele excitedly.

'No; that is the dreadful part of it,' answered the artist; 'on the open hillside where the boy had been standing a second ago, stood a large wolf, blackish in colour, with gleaming fangs and cruel, yellow eyes. You may think –'

But Van Cheele did not stop for anything as futile as thought. Already he was tearing at top speed towards the station. He dismissed the idea of a telegram. 'Gabriel-Ernest is a werewolf' was a hopelessly inadequate effort at conveying the situation, and his aunt would think it was a code message to which he had omitted to give her the key. His one hope was that he might reach home before sundown. The cab which he chartered at the other end of the railway journey bore him with what seemed exasperating slowness along the country roads, which were pink and mauve with the flush of the sinking sun. His aunt was putting away some unfinished jams and cake when he arrived.

'Where is Gabriel-Ernest?' he almost screamed.

'He is taking the little Toop child home,' said his aunt. 'It was getting so late, I thought it wasn't safe to let it go back alone. What a lovely sunset, isn't it?'

But Van Cheele, although not oblivious of the glow in the western sky, did not stay to discuss its beauties. At a speed for which he was scarcely geared he raced along the narrow lane that led to the home of the Toops. On one side ran the swift current of the millstream, on the other rose the stretch of bare hillside. A dwindling rim of red sun showed still on the skyline, and the next turning must bring him in view of the ill-assorted couple he was pursuing. Then the colour went suddenly out of things, and a grey light settled itself with a quick shiver over the landscape. Van Cheele heard a shrill wail of fear, and stopped running.

Nothing was ever seen again of the Toop child or Gabriel-Ernest, but the latter's discarded garments were found lying in the road, so it was assumed that the child had fallen into the water, and that the boy had stripped and jumped in, in a vain endeavour to save it. Van Cheele and some workmen who were near by at the time testified to having heard a child scream loudly just near the spot where the clothes were found. Mrs Toop, who had eleven other children, was decently resigned to her bereavement, but Miss Van Cheele sincerely mourned her lost foundling. It was on her initiative that a memorial brass was put up in the parish church to 'Gabriel-Ernest, an unknown boy, who bravely sacrificed his life for another.'

Van Cheele gave way to his aunt in most things, but he flatly refused to subscribe to the Gabriel-Ernest memorial.

Tobermory

It was a chill, rain-washed afternoon of a late August day, that indefinite season when partridges are still in security or cold storage, and there is nothing to hunt – unless one is bounded on the north by the Bristol Channel, in which case one may lawfully gallop after fat red stags. Lady Blemley's house-party was not bounded on the north by the Bristol Channel, hence there was a full gathering of her guests round the tea-table on this particular afternoon. And, in spite of the blankness of the season and the triteness of the occasion, there was no trace in the company of that fatigued restlessness which means a dread of the pianola and a subdued hankering for auction bridge. The undisguised open-mouthed attention of the entire party was fixed on the homely negative personality of Mr Cornelius Appin. Of all her guests, he was the one who had come to Lady Blemley with the vaguest reputation. Someone had said he was 'clever', and he had got his invitation in the moderate expectation, on the part of his hostess, that some portion at least of his cleverness would be contributed to the general entertainment. Until tea-time that day she had been unable to discover in what direction, if any, his cleverness lay. He was neither a wit nor a croquet champion, a hypnotic force nor a begetter of amateur theatricals. Neither did his exterior suggest the sort of man in whom women are willing to pardon a generous measure of mental deficiency. He had subsided into mere Mr Appin, and the Cornelius seemed a piece of transparent baptismal bluff. And now he was claiming to have launched on the world a discovery beside which the invention of gunpowder, of the printing-press, and of steam locomotion were inconsiderable trifles. Science had made bewildering strides in many directions during recent decades, but this thing seemed to belong to the domain of miracle rather than to scientific achievement.

'And do you really ask us to believe,' Sir Wilfrid was saying, 'that you have discovered a means for instructing animals in the art of human speech, and that dear old Tobermory has proved your first successful pupil?'

'It is a problem at which I have worked for the last seventeen years,' said Mr Appin, 'but only during the last eight or nine months have I been rewarded with glimmerings of success. Of course I have experimented with thousands of animals, but latterly only with cats, those wonderful creatures which have assimilated themselves so marvellously with our civilization while retaining all their highly developed feral instincts. Here and there among cats one comes across an outstanding superior intellect, just as one does among the ruck of human beings, and when I made the acquaintance of Tobermory a week ago I saw at once that I was in contact with a "Beyond-cat" of extraordinary intelligence. I had gone far along the road to success in recent experiments; with Tobermory, as you call him, I have reached the goal.'

Mr Appin concluded his remarkable statement in a voice which he strove to divest of a triumphant inflection. No one said 'Rats', though Clovis's lips moved in a mono-syllabic contortion which probably invoked those rodents of disbelief.

'And do you mean to say,' asked Miss Resker, after a slight pause, 'that you have taught Tobermory to say and understand easy sentences of one syllable?'

'My dear Miss Resker,' said the wonder-worker patiently, 'one teaches little children and savages and backward adults in that piecemeal fashion; when one has once solved the problem of making a beginning with an animal of highly developed intelligence one has no need for those halting methods. Tobermory can speak our language with perfect correctness.'

This time Clovis very distinctly said, 'Beyond-rats!' Sir Wilfrid was more polite, but equally sceptical.

'Hadn't we better have the cat in and judge for ourselves?' suggested Lady Blemley.

Sir Wilfrid went in search of the animal, and the company settled themselves down to the languid expectation of witnessing some more or less adroit drawing-room ventriloquism.

In a minute Sir Wilfrid was back in the room, his face white beneath its tan and his eyes dilated with excitement.

'By Gad, it's true!'

His agitation was unmistakably genuine, and his hearers started forward in a thrill of awakened interest.

Collapsing into an armchair he continued breathlessly: 'I found him dozing in the smoking-room and called out to him to come for his tea. He blinked at me in his usual way, and I said, "Come on, Toby; don't keep us waiting"; and, by Gad! he drawled out in a most horribly natural voice that he'd come when he dashed well pleased! I nearly jumped out of my skin!'

Appin had preached to absolutely incredulous hearers; Sir Wilfrid's statement carried instant conviction. A Babel-like chorus of startled exclamation arose, amid which the scientist sat mutely enjoying the first fruit of his stupendous discovery.

In the midst of the clamour Tobermory entered the room and made his way with velvet tread and studied unconcern across to the group seated round the tea-table.

A sudden hush of awkwardness and constraint fell on the company. Somehow there seemed an element of embarrassment in addressing on equal terms a domestic cat of acknowledged dental ability.

'Will you have some milk, Tobermory?' asked Lady Blemley in a rather strained voice.

'I don't mind if I do,' was the response, couched in a tone of even indifference. A shiver of suppressed excitement went through the listeners, and Lady Blemley might be excused for pouring out the saucerful of milk rather unsteadily.

'I'm afraid I've spilt a good deal of it,' she said apologetically.

'After all, it's not my Axminster,' was Tobermory's rejoinder.

Another silence fell on the group, and then Miss Resker, in her best district-visitor manner, asked if the human language had been difficult to learn. Tobermory looked squarely at her for a moment and then fixed his gaze serenely on the middle distance. It was obvious that boring questions lay outside his scheme of life.

'What do you think of human intelligence?' asked Mavis Pellington lamely.

'Of whose intelligence in particular?' asked Tobermory coldly.

'Oh, well, mine for instance,' said Mavis, with a feeble laugh.

'You put me in an embarrassing position,' said Tobermory, whose tone and attitude certainly did not suggest a shred of embarrassment. 'When your inclusion in this house-party was suggested Sir Wilfrid protested that you were the most brainless woman of his acquaintance, and

33

that there was a wide distinction between hospitality and the care of the feeble-minded. Lady Blemley replied that your lack of brain-power was the precise quality which had earned you your invitation, as you were the only person she could think of who might be idiotic enough to buy their old car. You know, the one they call "The Envy of Sisyphus", because it goes quite nicely up-hill if you push it.'

Lady Blemley's protestations would have had greater effect if she had not casually suggested to Mavis only that morning that the car in question would be just the thing for her down at her Devonshire home.

Major Barfield plunged in heavily to effect a diversion.

'How about your carryings-on with the tortoise-shell puss up at the stables, eh?'

The moment he had said it everyone realized the blunder.

'One does not usually discuss these matters in public,' said Tobermory frigidly. 'From a slight observation of your ways since you've been in this house I should imagine you'd find it inconvenient if I were to shift the conversation on to your own little affairs.'

The panic which ensued was not confined to the Major.

'Would you like to go and see if cook has got your dinner ready?' suggested Lady Blemley hurriedly, affecting to ignore the fact that it wanted at least two hours to Tobermory's dinner-time.

'Thanks,' said Tobermory, 'not quite so soon after my tea. I don't want to die of indigestion.'

'Cats have nine lives, you know,' said Sir Wilfrid heartily.

'Possibly,' answered Tobermory; 'but only one liver.'

'Adelaide!' said Mrs Cornett, 'do you mean to encourage that cat to go out and gossip about us in the servants' hall?'

The panic had indeed become general. A narrow ornamental balustrade ran in front of most of the bedroom windows at the Towers, and it was recalled with dismay that this had formed a favourite promenade for Tobermory at all hours, whence he could watch the pigeons – and heaven knew what else besides. If he intended to become reminiscent in his present outspoken strain the effect would be something more than disconcerting. Mrs Cornett, who spent much time at her toilet table, and whose complexion was reputed to be of a nomadic though punctual disposition, looked as ill at ease as the Major. Miss Scrawen, who wrote fiercely sensuous poetry and led a blameless life, merely displayed irritation; if you are methodical and virtuous in private you don't necessarily want every one to know it. Bertie van Tahn, who was so depraved at seventeen that he had long ago given up trying to be any worse, turned a dull shade of gardenia white, but he did not commit the error of dashing out of the room like Odo Finsberry, a young gentleman who was understood to be reading for the Church and who was possibly disturbed at the thought of scandals he might hear concerning other people. Clovis had the presence of mind to maintain a composed exterior; privately he was calculating how long it would take to procure a box of fancy mice through the agency of the *Exchange and Mart* as a species of hush-money.

Even in a delicate situation like the present, Agnes Resker could not endure to remain too long in the background.

'Why did I ever come down here?' she asked dramatically.

Tobermory immediately accepted the opening.

'Judging by what you said to Mrs Cornett on the croquet-lawn yesterday, you were out for food. You described the Blemleys as the dullest people to stay with that you knew, but said they were clever enough to employ a first-rate cook; otherwise they'd find it difficult to get anyone to come down a second time.'

'There's not a word of truth in it! I appeal to Mrs Cornett –' exclaimed the discomfited Agnes.

'Mrs Cornett repeated your remark afterwards to Bertie van Tahn,' continued Tobermory, 'and said, "That woman is a regular Hunger Marcher; she'd go anywhere for four square meals a day", and Bertie van Tahn said –'

At this point the chronicle mercifully ceased. Tobermory had caught a glimpse of the big yellow Tom from the Rectory working his way through the shrubbery towards the stable wing. In a flash he had vanished through the open French window.

With the disappearance of his too brilliant pupil Cornelius Appin found himself beset by a hurricane of bitter upbraiding, anxious inquiry, and frightened entreaty. The responsibility for the situation lay with him, and he must prevent matters from becoming worse. Could Tobermory impart his dangerous gift to other cats? was the first question he had to answer. It was possible, he replied, that he might have initiated his intimate friend the stable puss into his new accomplishment, but it was unlikely that his teaching could have taken a wider range as yet.

'Then,' said Mrs Cornett, 'Tobermory may be a valuable cat and a great pet; but I'm sure you'll agree, Adelaide, that both he and the stable cat must be done away with without delay.'

'You don't suppose I've enjoyed the last quarter of an hour, do you?' said Lady Blemley bitterly. 'My husband and I are very fond of Tobermory – at least, we were before this horrible accomplishment was infused into him; but now, of course, the only thing is to have him destroyed as soon as possible.'

'We can put some strychnine in the scraps he always gets at dinner-time,' said Sir Wilfrid, 'and I will go and drown the stable cat myself. The coachman will be very sore at losing his pet, but I'll say a very catching form of mange has broken out in both cats and we're afraid of its spreading to the kennels.'

'But my great discovery!' expostulated Mr Appin; 'after all my years of research and experiment –'

'You can go and experiment on the short-horns at the farm, who are under proper control,' said Mrs Cornett, 'or the elephants at the Zoological Gardens. They're said to be highly intelligent, and they have this recommendation, that they don't come creeping about our bedrooms and under chairs, and so forth.'

An archangel ecstatically proclaiming the Millennium, and then finding that it clashed unpardonably with Henley and would have to be indefinitely postponed, could hardly have felt more crestfallen than Cornelius Appin at the reception of his wonderful achievement. Public opinion, however, was against him – in fact, had the general voice been consulted on the subject it is probable that a strong minority vote would have been in favour of including him in the strychnine diet.

Defective train arrangements and a nervous desire to see matters brought to a finish prevented an immediate dispersal of the party, but dinner that evening was not a social success. Sir Wilfrid had had rather a trying time with the stable cat and subsequently with the coachman. Agnes Resker ostentatiously limited her repast to a morsel of dry toast, which she bit as though it were a personal enemy; while Mavis Pellington maintained a vindictive silence throughout the meal. Lady Blemley kept up a flow of what she hoped was conversation, but her attention was fixed on the doorway. A plateful of carefully dosed fish scraps was in readiness on the sideboard, but sweets and savoury and dessert went their way, and no Tobermory appeared either in the dining-room or kitchen.

The sepulchral dinner was cheerful compared with the subsequent vigil in the smoking-room. Eating and drinking had at least supplied a distraction and cloak to the prevailing embarrassment. Bridge was out of the question in the general tension of nerves and tempers, and after Odo Finsberry had given a lugubrious rendering of 'Mélisande in the Wood' to a frigid audience, music was tacitly avoided. At eleven the servants went to bed, announcing that the small window in the pantry had been left open as usual for Tobermory's private use. The guests read steadily through the current batch of magazines, and fell back gradually on the 'Badminton Library' and bound volumes of *Punch*. Lady Blemley made periodic visits to the pantry, returning each time with an expression of listless depression which forestalled questioning.

At two o'clock Clovis broke the dominating silence.

'He won't turn up tonight. He's probably in the local newspaper office at the present moment, dictating the first instalment of his reminiscences. Lady What's-her-name's book won't be in it. It will be the event of the day.'

Having made this contribution to the general cheerfulness, Clovis went to bed. At long intervals the various members of the house-party followed his example.

The servants taking round the early tea made a uniform announcement in reply to a uniform question. Tobermory had not returned.

Breakfast was, if anything, a more unpleasant function than dinner had been, but before its conclusion the situation was relieved. Tobermory's corpse was brought in from the shrubbery, where a gardener had just discovered it. From the bites on his throat and the yellow fur which coated his claws it was evident that he had fallen in unequal combat with the big Tom from the Rectory.

By midday most of the guests had quitted the Towers, and after lunch Lady Blemley had sufficiently recovered her spirits to write an extremely nasty letter to the Rectory about the loss of her valuable pet.

Tobermory had been Appin's one successful pupil, and he was destined to have no successor. A few weeks later an elephant in the Dresden Zoological Garden, which had shown no previous signs of irritability, broke loose and killed an Englishman who had apparently been teasing it. The victim's name was variously reported in the papers as Oppin and Eppelin, but his front name was faithfully rendered Cornelius.

'If he was trying German irregular verbs on the poor beast,' said Clovis, 'he deserved all he got.'

Mrs. Packletide's Tiger

It was Mrs Packletide's pleasure and intention that she should shoot a tiger. Not that the lust to kill had suddenly descended on her, or that she felt that she would leave India safer and more wholesome than she had found it, with one fraction less of wild beast per million of inhabitants. The compelling motive for her sudden deviation towards the footsteps of Nimrod was the fact that Loona Bimberton had recently been carried eleven miles in an aeroplane by an Algerian aviator, and talked of nothing else; only a personally procured tiger-skin and a heavy harvest of Press photographs could successfully counter that sort of thing. Mrs Packletide had already arranged in her mind the lunch she would give at her house in Curzon Street, ostensibly in Loona Bimberton's honour, with a tiger-skin rug occupying most of the foreground and all of the conversation. She had also already designed in her mind the tiger-claw brooch that she was going to give Loona Bimberton on her next birthday. In a world that is supposed to be chiefly swayed by hunger and by love Mrs Packletide was an exception; her movements and motives were largely governed by dislike of Loona Bimberton.

Circumstances proved propitious. Mrs Packletide had offered a thousand rupees for the opportunity of shooting a tiger without overmuch risk or exertion, and it so happened that a neighbouring village could boast of being the favoured rendezvous of an animal of respectable antecedents, which had been driven by the increasing infirmities of age to abandon game-killing and confine its appetite to the smaller domestic animals. The prospect of earning the thousand rupees had stimulated the sporting and commercial instinct of the villagers; children were posted night and day on the outskirts of the local jungle to head the tiger back in the unlikely event of his attempting to roam away to fresh hunting-grounds, and the cheaper kinds of goats were left about with elaborate carelessness to keep him satisfied with his present quarters. The one great anxiety was lest he should die of old age before the date appointed for the memsahib's shoot. Mothers carrying their babies home through the jungle after the day's work in the fields hushed their singing lest they might curtail the restful sleep of the venerable herd-robber.

The great night duly arrived, moonlit and cloudless. A platform had been constructed in a comfortable and conveniently placed tree, and thereon crouched Mrs Packletide and her paid companion, Miss Mebbin. A goat, gifted with a particularly persistent bleat, such as even a partially deaf tiger might be reasonably expected to hear on a still night, was tethered at the correct distance. With an accurately sighted rifle and a thumbnail pack of patience cards the sportswoman awaited the coming of the quarry.

'I suppose we are in some danger?' said Miss Mebbin.

She was not actually nervous about the wild beast, but she had a morbid dread of performing an atom more service than she had been paid for.

'Nonsense,' said Mrs Packletide; 'it's a very old tiger. It couldn't spring up here even if it wanted to.'

'If it's an old tiger I think you ought to get it cheaper. A thousand rupees is a lot of money.'

Louisa Mebbin adopted a protective elder-sister attitude towards money in general, irrespective of nationality or denomination. Her energetic intervention had saved many a rouble from dissipating itself in tips in some Moscow hotel, and francs and centimes clung to her instinctively under circumstances which would have driven them headlong from less sympathetic hands. Her speculations as to the market depreciation of tiger remnants were cut short by the appearance on the scene of the animal itself. As soon as it caught sight of the tethered goat it lay flat on the earth, seemingly less from a desire to take advantage of all available cover than for the purpose of snatching a short rest before commencing the grand attack.

43

'I believe it's ill,' said Louisa Mebbin, loudly in Hin-
dustani, for the benefit of the village headman, who was
in ambush in a neighbouring tree.

'Hush!' said Mrs Packletide, and at that moment the
tiger commenced ambling towards his victim.

'Now, now!' urged Miss Mebbin with some excitement; 'if he doesn't touch the goat we needn't pay for it.'
(The bait was an extra.)

The rifle flashed out with a loud report, and the great
tawny beast sprang to one side and then rolled over in
the stillness of death. In a moment a crowd of excited
natives had swarmed on to the scene, and their shouting
speedily carried the glad news to the village, where a
thumping of tom-toms took up the chorus of triumph.
And their triumph and rejoicing found a ready echo in
the heart of Mrs Packletide; already that luncheon-party
in Curzon Street seemed immeasurably nearer.

It was Louisa Mebbin who drew attention to the fact
that the goat was in death-throes from a mortal bullet-
wound, while no trace of the rifle's deadly work could be
found on the tiger. Evidently the wrong animal had been
hit, and the beast of prey had succumbed to heart-failure,
caused by the sudden report of the rifle, accelerated by
senile decay. Mrs Packletide was pardonably annoyed at
the discovery; but, at any rate, she was the possessor of
a dead tiger, and the villagers, anxious for their thousand
rupees, gladly connived at the fiction that she had shot
the beast. And Miss Mebbin was a paid companion.

Therefore did Mrs Packletide face the cameras with a light heart, and her pictured fame reached from the pages of the *Texas Weekly Snapshot* to the illustrated Monday supplement of the *Novoe Vremya*. As for Loona Bimberton, she refused to look at an illustrated paper for weeks, and her letter of thanks for the gift of a tiger-claw brooch was a model of repressed emotions. The luncheon-party she declined; there are limits beyond which repressed emotions become dangerous.

From Curzon Street the tiger-skin rug travelled down to the Manor House, and was duly inspected and admired by the county, and it seemed a fitting and appropriate thing when Mrs Packletide went to the County Costume Ball in the character of Diana. She refused to fall in, however, with Clovis's tempting suggestion of a primeval dance party, at which every one should wear the skins of beasts they had recently slain. 'I should be in rather a Baby Bunting condition,' confessed Clovis, 'with a miserable rabbit-skin or two to wrap up in, but then,' he added, with a rather malicious glance at Diana's proportions, 'my figure is quite as good as that Russian dancing boy's.'

'How amused every one would be if they knew what really happened,' said Louisa Mebbin a few days after the ball.

'What do you mean?' asked Mrs Packletide quickly.

'How you shot the goat and frightened the tiger to death,' said Miss Mebbin, with her disagreeably pleasant laugh.

'No one would believe it,' said Mrs Packletide, her face changing colour as rapidly as though it were going through a book of patterns before post-time.

'Loona Bimberton would,' said Miss Mebbin. Mrs Packletide's face settled on an unbecoming shade of greenish white.

'You surely wouldn't give me away?' she asked.

'I've seen a week-end cottage near Dorking that I should rather like to buy,' said Miss Mebbin with seeming irrelevance. 'Six hundred and eighty, freehold. Quite a bargain, only I don't happen to have the money.'

Louisa Mebbin's pretty week-end cottage, christened by her 'Les Fauves', and gay in summer-time with its garden borders of tiger-lilies, is the wonder and admiration of her friends.

'It is a marvel how Louisa manages to do it,' is the general verdict.

Mrs Packletide indulges in no more big-game shooting.

'The incidental expenses are so heavy,' she confides to inquiring friends.

The Stampeding of Lady Bastable

'It would be rather nice if you would put Clovis up for another six days while I go up north to the MacGregors',' said Mrs Sangrail sleepily across the breakfast-table. It was her invariable plan to speak in a sleepy, comfortable voice whenever she was unusually keen about anything; it put people off their guard, and they frequently fell in with her wishes before they had realized that she was really asking for anything. Lady Bastable, however, was not so easily taken unawares; possibly she knew that voice and what it betokened – at any rate, she knew Clovis.

She frowned at a piece of toast and ate it very slowly, as though she wished to convey the impression that the process hurt her more than it hurt the toast; but no extension of hospitality on Clovis's behalf rose to her lips.

'It would be a great convenience to me,' pursued Mrs Sangrail, abandoning the careless tone. 'I particularly don't want to take him to the MacGregors', and it will only be for six days.'

'It will seem longer,' said Lady Bastable dismally. 'The last time he stayed here for a week –'

'I know,' interrupted the other hastily, 'but that was nearly two years ago. He was younger then.'

'But he hasn't improved,' said her hostess; 'it's no use growing older if you only learn new ways of misbehaving yourself.'

Mrs Sangrail was unable to argue the point; since Clovis had reached the age of seventeen she had never ceased to bewail his irrepressible waywardness to all her circle of acquaintances, and a polite scepticism would have greeted the slightest hint at a prospective reformation. She discarded the fruitless effort at cajolery and resorted to undisguised bribery.

'If you'll have him here for these six days I'll cancel that outstanding bridge account.'

It was only for forty-nine shillings, but Lady Bastable loved shillings with a great, strong love. To lose money at bridge and not to have to pay it was one of those rare experiences which gave the card-table a glamour in her eyes which it could never otherwise have possessed. Mrs Sangrail was almost equally devoted to her card winnings, but the prospect of conveniently warehousing her off-spring for six days, and incidentally saving his railway fare to the north, reconciled her to the sacrifice; when Clovis made a belated appearance at the breakfast-table the bargain had been struck.

'Just think,' said Mrs Sangrail sleepily; 'Lady Bastable

has very kindly asked you to stay on here while I go to the MacGregors'.'

Clovis said suitable things in a highly unsuitable manner, and proceeded to make punitive expeditions among the breakfast dishes with a scowl on his face that would have driven the purr out of a peace conference. The arrangement that had been concluded behind his back was doubly distasteful to him. In the first place, he particularly wanted to teach the MacGregor boys, who could well afford the knowledge, how to play poker-patience; secondly, the Bastable catering was of the kind that is classified as a rude plenty, which Clovis translated as a plenty that gives rise to rude remarks. Watching him from behind ostentatiously sleepy lids, his mother realized, in the light of long experience, that any rejoicing over the success of her manœuvre would be distinctly premature. It was one thing to fit Clovis into a convenient niche of the domestic jigsaw puzzle; it was quite another matter to get him to stay there.

Lady Bastable was wont to retire in state to the morning-room immediately after breakfast and spend a quiet hour in skimming through the papers; they were there, so she might as well get their money's worth out of them. Politics did not greatly interest her, but she was obsessed with a favourite foreboding that one of these days there would be a great social upheaval, in which everybody would be killed by everybody else. 'It will come sooner than we think,' she would observe darkly;

a mathematical expert of exceptionally high powers would have been puzzled to work out the approximate date from the slender and confusing groundwork which this assertion afforded.

On this particular morning the sight of Lady Bastable enthroned among her papers gave Clovis the hint towards which his mind had been groping all breakfast time. His mother had gone upstairs to supervise packing operations, and he was alone on the ground-floor with his hostess – and the servants. The latter were the key to the situation. Bursting wildly into the kitchen quarters, Clovis screamed a frantic though strictly non-committal summons: 'Poor Lady Bastable! In the morning-room! Oh, quick!' The next moment the butler, cook, page-boy, two or three maids, and a gardener who had happened to be in one of the outer kitchens were following in a hot scurry after Clovis as he headed back for the morning-room. Lady Bastable was roused from the world of newspaper lore by hearing a Japanese screen in the hall go down with a crash. Then the door leading from the hall flew open and her young guest tore madly through the room, shrieked at her in passing, 'The jacquerie! They're on us!' and dashed like an escaping hawk out through the French window. The scared mob of servants burst in on his heels, the gardener still clutching the sickle with which he had been trimming hedges, and the impetus of their headlong haste carried them, slipping and sliding, over the smooth parquet flooring towards the chair where their mistress sat in panic-stricken amazement. If she had had a moment granted her for reflection she would have behaved, as she afterwards explained, with considerable dignity. It was probably the sickle which decided her, but anyway she followed the lead that Clovis had given her through the French window, and ran well and far across the lawn before the eyes of her astonished retainers.

Lost dignity is not a possession which can be restored at a moment's notice, and both Lady Bastable and the butler found the process of returning to normal conditions almost as painful as a slow recovery from drowning. A jacquerie, even if carried out with the most respectful of intentions, cannot fail to leave some traces of embarrassment behind it. By lunch-time, however, decorum had reasserted itself with enhanced rigour as a natural rebound from its recent overthrow, and the meal was served in a frigid stateliness that might have been framed on a Byzantine model. Half-way through its duration Mrs Sangrail was solemnly presented with an envelope lying on a silver salver. It contained a cheque for forty-nine shillings.

The MacGregor boys learned how to play poker-patience; after all, they could afford to.

The Background

'That woman's art-jargon tires me,' said Clovis to his journalist friend. 'She's so fond of talking of certain pictures as "growing on one", as though they were a sort of fungus.'

'That reminds me,' said the journalist, 'of the story of Henri Deplis. Have I ever told it you?'

Clovis shook his head.

'Henri Deplis was by birth a native of the Grand Duchy of Luxemburg. On maturer reflection he became a commercial traveller. His business activities frequently took him beyond the limits of the Grand Duchy, and he was stopping in a small town of Northern Italy when news reached him from home that a legacy from a distant and deceased relative had fallen to his share.

'It was not a large legacy, even from the modest standpoint of Henri Deplis, but it impelled him towards some seemingly harmless extravagances. In particular it led him to patronize local art as represented by the tattoo-needles of Signor Andreas Pincini. Signor Pincini was, perhaps, the most brilliant master of tattoo craft that Italy had ever known, but his circumstances were decidedly impoverished, and for the sum of six hundred francs he gladly undertook to cover his client's back, from the collar-bone down to the waist-line, with a glowing representation of the Fall of Icarus. The design, when finally developed, was a slight disappointment to Monsieur Deplis, who had suspected Icarus of being a fortress taken by Wallenstein in the Thirty Years' War, but he was more than satisfied with the execution of the work, which was acclaimed by all who had the privilege of seeing it as Pincini's masterpiece.

'It was his greatest effort, and his last. Without even waiting to be paid, the illustrious craftsman departed this life, and was buried under an ornate tombstone, whose winged cherubs would have afforded singularly little scope for the exercise of his favourite art. There remained, however, the widow Pincini, to whom the six hundred francs were due. And thereupon arose the great crisis in the life of Henri Deplis, traveller of commerce. The legacy, under the stress of numerous little calls on its substance, had dwindled to very insignificant proportions, and when a pressing wine bill and sundry other current accounts had been paid, there remained little more than 430 francs to offer to the widow. The lady was properly indignant, not wholly, as she volubly explained, on account of the suggested writing-off of 170 francs, but also at the attempt to depreciate the value of her late husband's acknowledged masterpiece. In a week's time Deplis was obliged to reduce his offer to 405 francs, which circumstance fanned the widow's indignation into a fury. She cancelled the sale of the work of art, and a few days later Deplis learned with a sense of consternation that she had presented it to the municipality of Bergamo, which had gratefully accepted it. He left the neighbourhood as unobtrusively as possible, and was genuinely relieved when his business commands took him to Rome, where he hoped his identity and that of the famous picture might be lost sight of.

'But he bore on his back the burden of the dead man's genius. On presenting himself one day in the steaming corridor of a vapour bath, he was at once hustled back into his clothes by the proprietor, who was a North Italian, and who emphatically refused to allow the celebrated Fall of Icarus to be publicly on view without the permission of the municipality of Bergamo. Public interest and official vigilance increased as the matter became more widely known, and Deplis was unable to take a simple dip in the sea or river on the hottest afternoon unless clothed up to the collar-bone in a substantial bathing garment. Later on the authorities of Bergamo conceived the idea that salt water might be injurious to the masterpiece, and a perpetual injunction was obtained which debarred the muchly harassed commercial traveller from sea bathing under any circumstances. Altogether, he was fervently thankful when his firm of employers found him a new range of activities in the neighbourhood of

Bordeaux. His thankfulness, however, ceased abruptly at the Franco-Italian frontier. An imposing array of official force barred his departure, and he was sternly reminded of the stringent law which forbids the exportation of Italian works of art.

'A diplomatic parley ensued between the Luxemburgian and Italian Governments, and at one time the European situation became overcast with the possibilities of trouble. But the Italian Government stood firm; it declined to concern itself in the least with the fortunes or even the existence of Henri Deplis, commercial traveller, but was immovable in its decision that the Fall of Icarus (by the late Pincini, Andreas) at present the property of the municipality of Bergamo, should not leave the country.

'The excitement died down in time, but the unfortunate Deplis, who was of a constitutionally retiring disposition, found himself a few months later once more the storm-centre of a furious controversy. A certain German art expert, who had obtained from the municipality of Bergamo permission to inspect the famous masterpiece, declared it to be a spurious Pincini, probably the work of some pupil whom he had employed in his declining years. The evidence of Deplis on the subject was obviously worthless, as he had been under the influence of the customary narcotics during the long process of pricking in the design. The editor of an Italian art journal refuted the contentions of the German expert and undertook to prove that his private life did not conform to any modern standard of decency. The whole of Italy and Germany were drawn into the dispute, and the rest of Europe was soon involved in the quarrel. There were stormy scenes in the Spanish Parliament, and the University of Copenhagen bestowed a gold medal on the German expert (afterwards sending a commission to examine his proofs on the spot), while two Polish schoolboys in Paris committed suicide to show what *they* thought of the matter.

'Meanwhile, the unhappy human background fared no better than before, and it was not surprising that he drifted into the ranks of Italian anarchists. Four times at least he was escorted to the frontier as a dangerous and undesirable foreigner, but he was always brought back as the Fall of Icarus (attributed to Pincini, Andreas, early Twentieth Century). And then one day, at an anarchist congress at Genoa, a fellow-worker, in the heat of debate, broke a phial full of corrosive liquid over his back. The red shirt that he was wearing mitigated the effects, but the Icarus was ruined beyond recognition. His assailant was severely reprimanded for assaulting a fellow-anarchist and received seven years' imprisonment for defacing a national art treasure. As soon as he was able to leave the hospital Henri Deplis was put across the frontier as an undesirable alien.

'In the quieter streets of Paris, especially in the neighbourhood of the Ministry of Fine Arts, you may sometimes meet a depressed, anxious-looking man, who, if you pass him the time of day, will answer you with a slight Luxemburgian accent. He nurses the illusion that he is one of the lost arms of the Venus de Milo, and hopes that the French Government may be persuaded to buy him. On all other subjects I believe he is tolerably sane.'

The Jesting of Arlington Stringham

Arlington Stringham made a joke in the House of Commons. It was a thin House, and a very thin joke; something about the Anglo-Saxon race having a great many angles. It is possible that it was unintentional, but a fellow-member, who did not wish it to be supposed that he was asleep because his eyes were shut, laughed. One or two of the papers noted 'a laugh' in brackets, and another, which was notorious for the carelessness of its political news, mentioned 'laughter'. Things often begin in that way.

'Arlington made a joke in the House last night,' said Eleanor Stringham to her mother; 'in all the years we've been married neither of us has made jokes, and I don't like it now. I'm afraid it's the beginning of the rift in the lute.'

'What lute?' said her mother.

'It's a quotation,' said Eleanor.

To say that anything was a quotation was an excellent method, in Eleanor's eyes, for withdrawing it from discussion, just as you could always defend indifferent lamb late in the season by saying 'It's mutton.'

And, of course, Arlington Stringham continued to tread the thorny path of conscious humour into which Fate had beckoned him.

'The country's looking very green, but, after all, that's what it's there for,' he remarked to his wife two days later.

'That's very modern, and I daresay very clever, but I'm afraid it's wasted on me,' she observed coldly. If she had known how much effort it had cost him to make the remark she might have greeted it in a kinder spirit. It is the tragedy of human endeavour that it works so often unseen and unguessed.

Arlington said nothing, not from injured pride, but because he was thinking hard for something to say. Eleanor mistook his silence for an assumption of tolerant superiority, and her anger prompted her to a further gibe.

'You had better tell it to Lady Isobel. I've no doubt she would appreciate it.'

Lady Isobel was seen everywhere with a fawn-coloured collie at a time when everyone else kept nothing but Pekinese, and she had once eaten four green apples at an afternoon tea in the Botanical Gardens, so she was widely credited with a rather unpleasant wit. The censorious said she slept in a hammock and understood Yeats's poems, but her family denied both stories.

'The rift is widening to an abyss,' said Eleanor to her mother that afternoon.

'I should not tell that to anyone,' remarked her mother, after long reflection.

'Naturally, I should not talk about it very much,' said Eleanor, 'but why shouldn't I mention it to anyone?'

'Because you can't have an abyss in a lute. There isn't room.'

Eleanor's outlook on life did not improve as the afternoon wore on. The page-boy had brought from the library *By Mere and Wold* instead of *By Mere Chance*, the book which everyone denied having read. The unwelcome substitute appeared to be a collection of nature notes contributed by the author to the pages of some Northern weekly, and when one had been prepared to plunge with disapproving mind into a regrettable chronicle of ill-spent lives it was intensely irritating to read 'the dainty yellow-hammers are now with us, and flaunt their jaundiced livery from every bush and hillock.' Besides, the thing was so obviously untrue; either there must be hardly any bushes or hillocks in those parts or the country must be fearfully overstocked with yellow-hammers. The thing scarcely seemed worth telling such a lie about. And the page-boy stood there, with his sleekly brushed and parted hair, and his air of chaste and callous indifference to the desires and passions of the world. Eleanor hated boys, and she would have liked to have whipped this one long and often. It was perhaps the yearning of a woman who had no children of her own.

She turned at random to another paragraph. 'Lie quietly concealed in the fern and bramble in the gap by the old rowan tree, and you may see, almost every evening during early summer, a pair of lesser whitethroats creeping up and down the nettles and hedge-growth that mask their nesting-place.'

The insufferable monotony of the proposed recreation! Eleanor would not have watched the most brilliant performance at His Majesty's Theatre for a single evening under such uncomfortable circumstances, and to be asked to watch lesser whitethroats creeping up and down a nettle 'almost every evening' during the height of the season struck her as an imputation on her intelligence that was positively offensive. Impatiently she transferred her attention to the dinner menu, which the boy had thoughtfully brought in as an alternative to the more solid literary fare. 'Rabbit curry' met her eye, and the lines of disapproval deepened on her already puckered brow. The cook was a great believer in the influence of environment, and nourished an obstinate conviction that if you brought rabbit and curry-powder together in one dish a rabbit curry would be the result. And Clovis and the odious Bertie van Tahn were coming to dinner. Surely, thought Eleanor, if Arlington knew how much she had had that day to try her, he would refrain from joke-making.

At dinner that night it was Eleanor herself who mentioned the name of a certain statesman, who may be decently covered under the disguise of X.

'X.,' said Arlington Stringham, 'has the soul of a meringue.'

It was a useful remark to have on hand, because it applied equally well to four prominent statesmen of the day, which quadrupled the opportunities for using it.

'Meringues haven't got souls,' said Eleanor's mother.

'It's a mercy that they haven't,' said Clovis; 'they would be always losing them, and people like my aunt would get up missions to meringues, and say it was wonderful how much one could teach them and how much more one could learn from them.'

'What could you learn from a meringue?' asked Eleanor's mother.

'My aunt has been known to learn humility from an ex-Viceroy,' said Clovis.

'I wish cook would learn to make curry, or have the sense to leave it alone,' said Arlington, suddenly and savagely.

Eleanor's face softened. It was like one of his old remarks in the days when there was no abyss between them.

It was during the debate on the Foreign Office vote that Stringham made his great remark that 'the people of Crete unfortunately make more history than they can consume locally.' It was not brilliant, but it came in the middle of a dull speech, and the House was quite pleased with it. Old gentlemen with bad memories said it reminded them of Disraeli.

It was Eleanor's friend, Gertrude Ilpton, who drew her attention to Arlington's newest outbreak. Eleanor in these days avoided the morning papers.

'It's very modern, and I suppose very clever,' she observed.

'Of course it's clever,' said Gertrude; 'all Lady Isobel's sayings are clever, and luckily they bear repeating.'

'Are you sure it's one of her sayings?' asked Eleanor.

'My dear, I've heard her say it dozens of times.'

'So that is where he gets his humour,' said Eleanor slowly, and the hard lines deepened round her mouth.

The death of Eleanor Stringham from an overdose of chloral, occurring at the end of a rather uneventful season, excited a certain amount of unobtrusive speculation. Clovis, who perhaps exaggerated the importance of curry in the home, hinted at domestic sorrow.

And of course Arlington never knew. It was the tragedy of his life that he should miss the fullest effect of his jesting.

Sredni Vashtar

Conradin was ten years old, and the doctor had pronounced his professional opinion that the boy would not
live another five years. The doctor was silky and effete,
and counted for little, but his opinion was endorsed by
Mrs De Ropp, who counted for nearly everything. Mrs
De Ropp was Conradin's cousin and guardian, and in his
eyes she represented those three-fifths of the world that
are necessary and disagreeable and real; the other two-
fifths, in perpetual antagonism to the foregoing, were
summed up in himself and his imagination. One of these
days Conradin supposed he would succumb to the mas-
tering pressure of wearisome necessary things – such as
illnesses and coddling restrictions and drawn-out dulness.
Without his imagination, which was rampant under the
spur of loneliness, he would have succumbed long ago.

Mrs De Ropp would never, in her honestest moments,
have confessed to herself that she disliked Conradin,
though she might have been dimly aware that thwarting
him 'for his good' was a duty which she did not find

particularly irksome. Conradin hated her with a desperate sincerity which he was perfectly able to mask. Such few pleasures as he could contrive for himself gained an added relish from the likelihood that they would be displeasing to his guardian, and from the realm of his imagination she was locked out – an unclean thing, which should find no entrance.

In the dull, cheerless garden, overlooked by so many windows that were ready to open with a message not to do this or that, or a reminder that medicines were due, he found little attraction. The few fruit-trees that it contained were set jealously apart from his plucking, as though they were rare specimens of their kind blooming in an arid waste; it would probably have been difficult to find a market-gardener who would have offered ten shillings for their entire yearly produce. In a forgotten corner, however, almost hidden behind a dismal shrubbery, was a disused tool-shed of respectable proportions, and within its walls Conradin found a haven, something that took on the varying aspects of a playroom and a cathedral. He had peopled it with a legion of familiar phantoms, evoked partly from fragments of history and partly from his own brain, but it also boasted two inmates of flesh and blood. In one corner lived a ragged-plumaged Houdan hen, on which the boy lavished an affection that had scarcely another outlet. Further back in the gloom stood a large hutch, divided into two compartments, one of which was fronted with close iron bars. This was the abode of a large polecat-ferret, which a friendly butcher-boy had once smuggled, cage and all, into its present quarters, in exchange for a long-secreted hoard of small silver. Conradin was dreadfully afraid of the lithe, sharp-fanged beast, but it was his most treasured possession. Its very presence in the tool-shed was a secret and fearful joy, to be kept scrupulously from the knowledge of the Woman, as he privately dubbed his cousin. And one day, out of Heaven knows what material, he spun the beast a wonderful name, and from that moment it grew into a god and a religion. The Woman indulged in religion once a week at a church near by, and took Conradin with her, but to him the church service was an alien rite in the House of Rimmon. Every Thursday, in the dim and musty silence of the tool-shed, he worshipped with mystic and elaborate ceremonial before the wooden hutch where dwelt Sredni Vashtar, the great ferret. Red flowers in their season and scarlet berries in the winter-time were offered at his shrine, for he was a god who laid some special stress on the fierce impatient side of things, as opposed to the Woman's religion, which, as far as Conradin could observe, went to great lengths in the contrary direction. And on great festivals powdered nutmeg was strewn in front of his hutch, an important feature of the offering being that the nutmeg had to be stolen. These festivals were of irregular occurrence, and were chiefly appointed to celebrate some passing event. On one occasion, when

Mrs De Ropp suffered from acute toothache for three days, Conradin kept up the festival during the entire three days, and almost succeeded in persuading himself that Sredni Vashtar was personally responsible for the toothache. If the malady had lasted for another day the supply of nutmeg would have given out.

The Houdan hen was never drawn into the cult of Sredni Vashtar. Conradin had long ago settled that she was an Anabaptist. He did not pretend to have the remotest knowledge as to what an Anabaptist was, but he privately hoped that it was dashing and not very respectable. Mrs De Ropp was the ground plan on which he based and detested all respectability.

After a while Conradin's absorption in the tool-shed began to attract the notice of his guardian. 'It is not good for him to be pottering down there in all weathers,' she promptly decided, and at breakfast one morning she announced that the Houdan hen had been sold and taken away overnight. With her short-sighted eyes she peered at Conradin, waiting for an outbreak of rage and sorrow, which she was ready to rebuke with a flow of excellent precepts and reasoning. But Conradin said nothing: there was nothing to be said. Something perhaps in his white set face gave her a momentary qualm, for at tea that afternoon there was toast on the table, a delicacy which she usually banned on the ground that it was bad for him; also because the making of it 'gave trouble', a deadly offence in the middle-class feminine eye.

'I thought you liked toast,' she exclaimed, with an injured air, observing that he did not touch it.

'Sometimes,' said Conradin.

In the shed that evening there was an innovation in the worship of the hutch-god. Conradin had been wont to chant his praises, tonight he asked a boon.

'Do one thing for me, Sredni Vashtar.'

The thing was not specified. As Sredni Vashtar was a god he must be supposed to know. And choking back a sob as he looked at that other empty corner, Conradin went back to the world he so hated.

And every night, in the welcome darkness of his bedroom, and every evening in the dusk of the tool-shed, Conradin's bitter litany went up: 'Do one thing for me, Sredni Vashtar.'

Mrs De Ropp noticed that the visits to the shed did not cease, and one day she made a further journey of inspection.

'What are you keeping in that locked hutch?' she asked. 'I believe it's guinea-pigs. I'll have them all cleared away.'

Conradin shut his lips tight, but the Woman ransacked his bedroom till she found the carefully hidden key, and forthwith marched down to the shed to complete her discovery. It was a cold afternoon, and Conradin had been bidden to keep to the house. From the furthest window of the dining-room the door of the shed could just be seen beyond the corner of the shrubbery, and there

Conradin stationed himself. He saw the Woman enter, and then he imagined her opening the door of the sacred hutch and peering down with her short-sighted eyes into the thick straw bed where his god lay hidden. Perhaps she would prod at the straw in her clumsy impatience. And Conradin fervently breathed his prayer for the last time. But he knew as he prayed that he did not believe. He knew that the Woman would come out presently with that pursed smile he loathed so well on her face, and that in an hour or two the gardener would carry away his wonderful god, a god no longer, but a simple brown ferret in a hutch. And he knew that the Woman would triumph always as she triumphed now, and that he would grow ever more sickly under her pestering and domineering and superior wisdom, till one day nothing would matter much more with him, and the doctor would be proved right. And in the sting and misery of his defeat, he began to chant loudly and defiantly the hymn of his threatened idol:

> Sredni Vashtar went forth,
> His thoughts were red thoughts and his teeth were white.
> His enemies called for peace, but he brought them death.
> Sredni Vashtar the Beautiful.

And then of a sudden he stopped his chanting and drew closer to the window-pane. The door of the shed still stood ajar as it had been left, and the minutes were slipping by. They were long minutes, but they slipped by nevertheless. He watched the starlings running and flying in little parties across the lawn; he counted them over and over again, with one eye always on that swinging door. A sour-faced maid came in to lay the table for tea, and still Conradin stood and waited and watched. Hope had crept by inches into his heart, and now a look of triumph began to blaze in his eyes that had only known the wistful patience of defeat. Under his breath, with a furtive exultation, he began once again the pæan of victory and devastation. And presently his eyes were rewarded: out through that doorway came a long, low, yellow-and-brown beast, with eyes a-blink at the waning daylight, and dark wet stains around the fur of jaws and throat. Conradin dropped on his knees. The great polecat-ferret made its way down to a small brook at the foot of the garden, drank for a moment, then crossed a little plank bridge and was lost to sight in the bushes. Such was the passing of Sredni Vashtar.

'Tea is ready,' said the sour-faced maid; 'where is the mistress?'

'She went down to the shed some time ago,' said Conradin.

And while the maid went to summon her mistress to tea, Conradin fished a toasting-fork out of the sideboard drawer and proceeded to toast himself a piece of bread. And during the toasting of it and the buttering of it with much butter and the slow enjoyment of eating it, Conradin listened to the noises and silences which fell in quick spasms beyond the dining-room door. The loud foolish screaming of the maid, the answering chorus of wondering ejaculations from the kitchen region, the scuttering footsteps and hurried embassies for outside help, and then, after a lull, the scared sobbings and the shuffling tread of those who bore a heavy burden into the house.

'Whoever will break it to the poor child? I couldn't for the life of me!' exclaimed a shrill voice. And while they debated the matter among themselves, Conradin made himself another piece of toast.

Adrian

A chapter in acclimatization

His baptismal register spoke of him pessimistically as
John Henry, but he had left that behind with the other
maladies of infancy, and his friends knew him under the
front-name of Adrian. His mother lived in Bethnal Green,
which was not altogether his fault; one can discourage
too much history in one's family, but one cannot always
prevent geography. And, after all, the Bethnal Green
habit has this virtue – that it is seldom transmitted to the
next generation. Adrian lived in a roomlet which came
under the auspicious constellation of W.

How he lived was to a great extent a mystery even to
himself; his struggle for existence probably coincided in
many material details with the rather dramatic accounts
he gave of it to sympathetic acquaintances. All that is
definitely known is that he now and then emerged from
the struggle to dine at the Ritz or Carlton, correctly
garbed and with a correctly critical appetite. On these

occasions he was usually the guest of Lucas Croyden, an amiable worldling, who had three thousand a year and a taste for introducing impossible people to irreproachable cookery. Like most men who combine three thousand a year with an uncertain digestion, Lucas was a Socialist, and he argued that you cannot hope to elevate the masses until you have brought plovers' eggs into their lives and taught them to appreciate the difference between coupe Jacques and Macédoine de fruits. His friends pointed out that it was a doubtful kindness to initiate a boy from behind a drapery counter into the blessedness of the higher catering, to which Lucas invariably replied that all kindnesses were doubtful. Which was perhaps true.

It was after one of his Adrian evenings that Lucas met his aunt, Mrs Mebberley, at a fashionable teashop, where the lamp of family life is still kept burning and you meet relatives who might otherwise have slipped your memory.

'Who was that good-looking boy who was dining with you last night?' she asked. 'He looked much too nice to be thrown away upon you.'

Susan Mebberley was a charming woman, but she was also an aunt.

'Who are his people?' she continued, when the protégés name (revised version) had been given her.

'His mother lives at Beth –'

Lucas checked himself on the threshold of what was perhaps a social indiscretion.

'Beth? Where is it? It sounds like Asia Minor. Is she mixed up with Consular people?'

'Oh, no. Her work lies among the poor.'

This was a side-slip into truth. The mother of Adrian was employed in a laundry.

'I see,' said Mrs Mebberley, 'mission work of some sort. And meanwhile the boy has no one to look after him. It's obviously my duty to see that he doesn't come to harm. Bring him to call on me.'

'My dear Aunt Susan,' expostulated Lucas, 'I really know very little about him. He may not be at all nice, you know, on further acquaintance.'

'He has delightful hair and a weak mouth. I shall take him with me to Homburg or Cairo.'

'It's the maddest thing I ever heard of,' said Lucas angrily.

'Well, there is a strong strain of madness in our family. If you haven't noticed it yourself all your friends must have.'

'One is so dreadfully under everybody's eyes at Homburg. At least you might give him a preliminary trial at Etretat.'

'And be surrounded by Americans trying to talk French? No, thank you. I love Americans, but not when they try to talk French. What a blessing it is that they never try to talk English. Tomorrow at five you can bring your young friend to call on me.'

And Lucas, realizing that Susan Mebberley was a

woman as well as an aunt, saw that she would have to be allowed to have her own way.

Adrian was duly carried abroad under the Mebberley wing; but as a reluctant concession to sanity Homburg and other inconveniently fashionable resorts were given a wide berth, and the Mebberley establishment planted itself down in the best hotel at Dohledorf, an Alpine townlet somewhere at the back of the Engadine. It was the usual kind of resort, with the usual type of visitors, that one finds over the greater part of Switzerland during the summer season, but to Adrian it was all unusual. The mountain air, the certainty of regular and abundant meals, and in particular the social atmosphere, affected him much as the indiscriminating fervour of a forcing-house might affect a weed that had strayed within its limits. He had been brought up in a world where break-ages were regarded as crimes and expiated as such; it was something new and altogether exhilarating to find that you were considered rather amusing if you smashed things in the right manner and at the recognized hours. Susan Mebberley had expressed the intention of showing Adrian a bit of the world; the particular bit of the world represented by Dohledorf began to be shown a good deal of Adrian.

Lucas got occasional glimpses of the Alpine sojourn, not from his aunt or Adrian, but from the industrious pen of Clovis, who was also moving as a satellite in the Mebberley constellation.

'The entertainment which Susan got up last night ended in disaster. I thought it would. The Grobmayer child, a particularly loathsome five-year-old, had appeared as "Bubbles" during the early part of the evening, and been put to bed during the interval. Adrian watched his opportunity and kidnapped it when the nurse was downstairs, and introduced it during the second half of the entertainment, thinly disguised as a performing pig. It certainly *looked* very like a pig, and grunted and slobbered just like the real article; no one knew exactly what it was, but every one said it was awfully clever, especially the Grobmayers. At the third curtain Adrian pinched it too hard, and it yelled "Marmar"! I am supposed to be good at descriptions, but don't ask me to describe the sayings and doings of the Grobmayers at that moment; it was like one of the angrier Psalms set to Strauss's music. We have moved to an hotel higher up the valley.'

Clovis's next letter arrived five days later, and was written from the Hotel Steinbock.

'We left the Hotel Victoria this morning. It was fairly comfortable and quiet – at least there was an air of repose about it when we arrived. Before we had been in residence twenty-four hours most of the repose had vanished "like a dutiful bream," as Adrian expressed it. However, nothing unduly outrageous happened till last night, when Adrian had a fit of insomnia and amused himself by unscrewing and transposing all the bedroom numbers on his floor. He transferred the bathroom label to the adjoining bedroom door, which happened to be that of Frau Hofrath Schilling, and this morning from seven o'clock onwards the old lady had a stream of involuntary visitors; she was too horrified and scandalized it seems to get up and lock her door. The would-be bathers flew back in confusion to their rooms, and, of course, the change of numbers led them astray again, and the corridor gradually filled with panic-stricken, scantily robed humans, dashing wildly about like rabbits in a ferret-infested warren. It took nearly an hour before the guests were all sorted into their respective rooms, and the Frau Hofrath's condition was still causing some anxiety when we left. Susan is beginning to look a little worried. She can't very well turn the boy adrift, as he hasn't got any money, and she can't send him to his people as she doesn't know where they are. Adrian says his mother moves about a good deal and he's lost her address. Probably, if the truth were known, he's had a row at home. So many boys nowadays seem to think that quarrelling with one's family is a recognized occupation.'

Lucas's next communication from the travellers took the form of a telegram from Mrs Mebberley herself. It was sent 'reply prepaid', and consisted of a single sentence: 'In Heaven's name, where is Beth?'

The Chaplet

A strange stillness hung over the restaurant; it was one of those rare moments when the orchestra was not discoursing the strains of the Ice-cream Sailor waltz.

'Did I ever tell you,' asked Clovis of his friend, 'the tragedy of music at mealtimes?

'It was a gala evening at the Grand Sybaris Hotel, and a special dinner was being served in the Amethyst dining-hall. The Amethyst dining-hall had almost a European reputation, especially with that section of Europe which is historically identified with the Jordan Valley. Its cooking was beyond reproach, and its orchestra was sufficiently highly salaried to be above criticism. Thither came in shoals the intensely musical and the almost intensely musical, who are very many, and in still greater numbers the merely musical, who know how Tschaikowsky's name is pronounced and can recognize several of Chopin's nocturnes if you give them due warning; these eat in the nervous, detached manner of roebuck feeding in the open, and keep anxious ears cocked towards the orchestra for the first hint of a recognizable melody.

'"Ah, yes, Pagliacci," they murmur, as the opening strains follow hot upon the soup, and if no contradiction is forthcoming from any better-informed quarter they break forth into subdued humming by way of supplementing the efforts of the musicians. Sometimes the melody starts on level terms with the soup, in which case the banqueters contrive somehow to hum between the spoonfuls; the facial expression of enthusiasts who are punctuating potage St Germain with Pagliacci is not beautiful, but it should be seen by those who are bent on observing all sides of life. One cannot discount the unpleasant things of this world merely by looking the other way.

'In addition to the aforementioned types the restaurant was patronized by a fair sprinkling of the absolutely non-musical; their presence in the dining-hall could only be explained on the supposition that they had come there to dine.

'The earlier stages of the dinner had worn off. The wine lists had been consulted, by some with the blank embarrassment of a schoolboy suddenly called on to locate a Minor Prophet in the tangled hinterland of the Old Testament, by others with the severe scrutiny which suggests that they have visited most of the higher-priced wines in their own homes and probed their family weaknesses. The diners who chose their wine in the latter fashion always gave their orders in a penetrating voice, with a plentiful garnishing of stage directions. By insisting on having your bottle pointing to the north when the cork is being drawn, and calling the waiter Max, you may induce an impression on your guests which hours of laboured boasting might be powerless to achieve. For this purpose, however, the guests must be chosen as carefully as the wine.

'Standing aside from the revellers in the shadow of a massive pillar was an interested spectator who was assuredly of the feast, and yet not in it. Monsieur Aristide Saucourt was the *chef* of the Grand Sybaris Hotel, and if he had an equal in his profession he had never acknowledged the fact. In his own domain he was a potentate, hedged around with the cold brutality that Genius expects rather than excuses in her children; he never forgave, and those who served him were careful that there should be little to forgive. In the outer world, the world which devoured his creations, he was an influence; how profound or how shallow an influence he never attempted to guess. It is the penalty and the safeguard of genius that it computes itself by troy weight in a world that measures by vulgar hundredweights.

'Once in a way the great man would be seized with a desire to watch the effect of his master-efforts, just as the guiding brain of Krupp's might wish at a supreme moment to intrude into the firing line of an artillery duel. And such an occasion was the present. For the first time in the history of the Grand Sybaris Hotel, he was presenting to its guests the dish which he had brought to that pitch of perfection which almost amounts to scandal. Canetons à la mode d'Amblève. In thin gilt lettering on the creamy white of the menu how little those words conveyed to the bulk of the imperfectly educated diners. And yet how much specialized effort had been lavished, how much carefully treasured lore had been ungarnered, before those six words could be written. In the Department of Deux-Sèvres ducklings had lived peculiar and beautiful lives and died in the odour of satiety to furnish the main theme of the dish; champignons, which even a purist for Saxon English would have hesitated to address as mushrooms, had contributed their languorous atrophied bodies to the garnishing, and a sauce devised in the twilight reign of the Fifteenth Louis had been summoned back from the imperishable past to take its part in the wonderful confection. Thus far had human effort laboured to achieve the desired result; the rest had been left to human genius – the genius of Aristide Saucourt.

'And now the moment had arrived for the serving of the great dish, the dish which world-weary Grand Dukes and market-obsessed money magnates counted among their happiest memories. And at the same moment something else happened. The leader of the highly salaried orchestra placed his violin caressingly against his chin, lowered his eyelids, and floated into a sea of melody.

'"Hark!" said most of the diners, "he is playing 'The Chaplet.'"

'They knew it was "The Chaplet" because they had heard it played at luncheon and afternoon tea, and at supper the night before, and had not had time to forget.

' "Yes, he is playing 'The Chaplet,' " they reassured one another. The general voice was unanimous on the subject. The orchestra had already played it eleven times that day, four times by desire and seven times from force of habit, but the familiar strains were greeted with the rapture due to a revelation. A murmur of much humming rose from half the tables in the room, and some of the more overwrought listeners laid down knife and fork in order to be able to burst in with loud clappings at the earliest permissible moment.

'And the Canetons à la mode d'Amblève? In stupefied, sickened wonder Aristide watched them grow cold in total neglect, or suffer the almost worse indignity of perfunctory pecking and listless munching while the banqueters lavished their approval and applause on the music-makers. Calves' liver and bacon, with parsley sauce, could hardly have figured more ignominiously in the evening's entertainment. And while the master of culinary art leaned back against the sheltering pillar, choking with a horrible brain-searing rage that could find no outlet for its agony, the orchestra leader was bowing his acknowledgments of the hand-clappings that rose in a storm around him. Turning to his colleagues he nodded the signal for an encore. But before the violin had been lifted anew into position there came from the shadow of the pillar an explosive negative.

'"Noh! Noh! You do not play thot again!"

'The musician turned in furious astonishment. Had he taken warning from the look in the other man's eyes he might have acted differently. But the admiring plaudits were ringing in his ears, and he snarled out sharply, "That is for me to decide."

'"Noh! You play thot never again," shouted the *chef*, and the next moment he had flung himself violently upon the loathed being who had supplanted him in the world's esteem. A large metal tureen, filled to the brim with steaming soup, had just been placed on a side table in readiness for a late party of diners; before the waiting staff or the guests had time to realize what was happening, Aristide had dragged his struggling victim up to the table and plunged his head deep down into the almost boiling contents of the tureen. At the further end of the room the diners were still spasmodically applauding in view of an encore.

'Whether the leader of the orchestra died from drowning by soup, or from the shock to his professional vanity, or was scalded to death, the doctors were never wholly able to agree. Monsieur Aristide Saucourt, who now lives in complete retirement, always inclined to the drowning theory.'

The Quest

An unwonted peace hung over the Villa Elsinore, broken, however, at frequent intervals, by clamorous lamentations suggestive of bewildered bereavement. The Momebys had lost their infant child; hence the peace which its absence entailed; they were looking for it in wild, undisciplined fashion, giving tongue the whole time, which accounted for the outcry which swept through house and garden whenever they returned to try the home coverts anew. Clovis, who was temporarily and unwillingly a paying guest at the villa, had been dozing in a hammock at the far end of the garden when Mrs Momeby had broken the news to him.

'We've lost Baby,' she screamed.

'Do you mean that it's dead, or stampeded, or that you staked it at cards and lost it that way?' asked Clovis lazily.

'He was toddling about quite happily on the lawn,' said Mrs Momeby tearfully, 'and Arnold had just come in, and I was asking him what sort of sauce he would like with the asparagus –'

'I hope he said hollandaise,' interrupted Clovis, with a show of quickened interest, 'because if there's anything I hate –'

'And all of a sudden I missed Baby,' continued Mrs Momeby in a shriller tone. 'We've hunted high and low, in house and garden and outside the gates, and he's nowhere to be seen.'

'Is he anywhere to be heard?' asked Clovis; 'if not, he must be at least two miles away.'

'But where? And how?' asked the distracted mother.

'Perhaps an eagle or a wild beast has carried him off,' suggested Clovis.

'There aren't eagles and wild beasts in Surrey,' said Mrs Momeby, but a note of horror had crept into her voice.

'They escape now and then from travelling shows. Sometimes I think they let them get loose for the sake of the advertisement. Think what a sensational headline it would make in the local papers: "Infant son of prominent Nonconformist devoured by spotted hyæna." Your husband isn't a prominent Nonconformist, but his mother came of Wesleyan stock, and you must allow the newspapers some latitude.'

'But we should have found his remains,' sobbed Mrs Momeby.

'If the hyæna was really hungry and not merely toying with his food there wouldn't be much in the way of remains. It would be like the small-boy-and-apple story – there ain't going to be no core.'

Mrs Momeby turned away hastily to seek comfort and counsel in some other direction. With the selfish absorption of young motherhood she entirely disregarded Clovis's obvious anxiety about the asparagus sauce. Before she had gone a yard, however, the click of the side gate caused her to pull up sharp. Miss Gilpet, from the Villa Peterhof, had come over to hear details of the bereavement. Clovis was already rather bored with the story, but Mrs Momeby was equipped with that merciless faculty which finds as much joy in the ninetieth time of telling as in the first.

'Arnold had just come in; he was complaining of rheumatism –'

'There are so many things to complain of in this household that it would never have occurred to me to complain of rheumatism,' murmured Clovis.

'He was complaining of rheumatism,' continued Mrs Momeby, trying to throw a chilling inflection into a voice that was already doing a good deal of sobbing and talking at high pressure as well.

She was again interrupted.

'There is no such thing as rheumatism,' said Miss Gilpet. She said it with the conscious air of defiance that a waiter adopts in announcing that the cheapest-priced claret in the wine-list is no more. She did not proceed, however, to offer the alternative of some more expensive malady, but denied the existence of them all.

Mrs Momeby's temper began to shine out through her grief.

'I suppose you'll say next that Baby hasn't really disappeared.'

'He has disappeared,' conceded Miss Gilpet, 'but only because you haven't sufficient faith to find him. It's only lack of faith on your part that prevents him from being restored to you safe and well.'

'But if he's been eaten in the meantime by a hyæna and partly digested,' said Clovis, who clung affectionately to his wild beast theory, 'surely some ill-effects would be noticeable?'

Miss Gilpet was rather staggered by this complication of the question.

'I feel sure that a hyæna has not eaten him,' she said lamely.

'The hyæna may be equally certain that it has. You see, it may have just as much faith as you have, and more special knowledge as to the present whereabouts of the baby.'

Mrs Momeby was in tears again. 'If you have faith,' she sobbed, struck by a happy inspiration, 'won't you find our little Erik for us? I am sure you have powers that are denied to us.'

Rose-Marie Gilpet was thoroughly sincere in her adherence to Christian Science principles; whether she understood or correctly expounded them the learned in such manners may best decide. In the present case she was undoubtedly confronted with a great opportunity, and as she started forth on her vague search she strenuously summoned to her aid every scrap of faith that she possessed. She passed out into the bare and open high road, followed by Mrs Momeby's warning, 'It's no use going there, we've searched there a dozen times.' But Rose-Marie's ears were already deaf to all things save self-congratulation; for sitting in the middle of the highway, playing contentedly with the dust and some faded buttercups, was a white-pinafored baby with a mop of tow-coloured hair tied over one temple with a pale-blue ribbon. Taking first the usual feminine precaution of looking to see that no motor-car was on the distant horizon, Rose-Marie dashed at the child and bore it, despite its vigorous opposition, in through the portals of Elsinore. The child's furious screams had already announced the fact of its discovery, and the almost hysterical parents raced down the lawn to meet their restored offspring. The aesthetic value of the scene was marred in some degree by Rose-Marie's difficulty in holding the struggling infant, which was borne wrong-end foremost towards the agitated bosom of its family. 'Our own little Erik come back to us,' cried the Momebys in unison; as the child had rammed its fists tightly into its eye-sockets and nothing could be seen of its face but a widely gaping mouth, the recognition was in itself almost an act of faith.

'Is he glad to get back to Daddy and Mummy again?' crooned Mrs Momeby; the preference which the child was showing for its dust and buttercup distractions was so marked that the question struck Clovis as being unnecessarily tactless.

'Give him a ride on the roly-poly,' suggested the father brilliantly, as the howls continued with no sign of early abatement. In a moment the child had been placed astride the big garden roller and a preliminary tug was given to set it in motion. From the hollow depths of the cylinder came an earsplitting roar, drowning even the vocal efforts of the squalling baby, and immediately afterwards there crept forth a white-pinafored infant with a mop of tow-coloured hair tied over one temple with a pale blue ribbon. There was no mistaking either the features or the lung-power of the new arrival.

'Our own little Erik,' screamed Mrs Momeby, pouncing on him and nearly smothering him with kisses; 'did he hide in the roly-poly to give us all a big fright?'

This was the obvious explanation of the child's sudden disappearance and equally abrupt discovery. There remained, however, the problem of the interloping baby, which now sat whimpering on the lawn in a disfavour as chilling as its previous popularity had been unwelcome. The Momebys glared at it as though it had wormed its way into their short-lived affections by heartless and unworthy pretences. Miss Gilpet's face took on an ashen tinge as she stared helplessly at the bunched-up figure that had been such a gladsome sight to her eyes a few moments ago.

'When love is over, how little of love even the lover understands,' quoted Clovis to himself.

Rose-Marie was the first to break the silence.

'If that is Erik you have in your arms, who is – that?'

'That, I think, is for you to explain,' said Mrs Momeby stiffly.

'Obviously,' said Clovis, 'it's a duplicate Erik that your powers of faith called into being. The question is: What are you going to do with him?'

The ashen pallor deepened in Rose-Marie's cheeks. Mrs Momeby clutched the genuine Erik closer to her side, as though she feared that her uncanny neighbour might out of sheer pique turn him into a bowl of gold-fish.

'I found him sitting in the middle of the road,' said Rose-Marie weakly.

'You can't take him back and leave him there,' said Clovis; 'the highway is meant for traffic, not to be used as a lumber-room for disused miracles.'

Rose-Marie wept. The proverb 'Weep and you weep alone' broke down as badly on application as most of its kind. Both babies were wailing lugubriously, and the parent Momebys had scarcely recovered from their earlier lachrymose condition. Clovis alone maintained an unruffled cheerfulness.

'Must I keep him always?' asked Rose-Marie dolefully.

'Not always,' said Clovis consolingly; 'he can go into the Navy when he's thirteen.' Rose-Marie wept afresh.

'Of course,' added Clovis, 'there may be no end of a bother about his birth certificate. You'll have to explain matters to the Admiralty, and they're dreadfully hidebound.'

It was rather a relief when a breathless nursemaid from the Villa Charlottenburg over the way came running across the lawn to claim little Percy, who had slipped out of the front gate and disappeared like a twinkling from the high road.

And even then Clovis found it necessary to go in person to the kitchen to make sure about the asparagus sauce.

Wratislav

The Gräfin's two elder sons had made deplorable marriages. It was, observed Clovis, a family habit. The
youngest boy, Wratislav, who was the black sheep of
a rather greyish family, had as yet made no marriage
at all.

'There is certainly this much to be said for viciousness,'
said the Gräfin, 'it keeps boys out of mischief.'

'Does it?' asked the Baroness Sophie, not by way of
questioning the statement, but with a painstaking effort
to talk intelligently. It was the one matter in which she
attempted to override the decrees of Providence, which
had obviously never intended that she should talk otherwise than inanely.

'I don't know why I shouldn't talk cleverly,' she would
complain; 'my mother was considered a brilliant
conversationalist.'

'These things have a way of skipping one generation,'
said the Gräfin.

'That seems so unjust,' said Sophie; 'one doesn't object

to one's mother having outshone one as a clever talker, but I must admit that I should be rather annoyed if my daughters talked brilliantly.'

'Well, none of them do,' said the Gräfin consolingly.

'I don't know about that,' said the Baroness, promptly veering round in defence of her offspring. 'Elsa said something quite clever on Thursday about the Triple Alliance. Something about it being like a paper umbrella, that was all right as long as you didn't take it out in the rain. It's not everyone who could say that.'

'Everyone has said it; at least everyone that I know. But then I know very few people.'

'I don't think you're particularly agreeable today.'

'I never am. Haven't you noticed that women with a really perfect profile like mine are seldom even moderately agreeable?'

'I don't think your profile is so perfect as all that,' said the Baroness.

'It would be surprising if it wasn't. My mother was one of the most noted classical beauties of her day.'

'These things sometimes skip a generation, you know,' put in the Baroness, with the breathless haste of one to whom repartee comes as rarely as the finding of a gold-handled umbrella.

'My dear Sophie,' said the Gräfin sweetly, 'that isn't in the least bit clever; but you do try so hard that I suppose I oughtn't to discourage you. Tell me something: has it ever occurred to you that Elsa would do very well for Wratislav? It's time he married somebody, and why not Elsa?'

'Elsa marry that dreadful boy!' gasped the Baroness.

'Beggars can't be choosers,' observed the Gräfin.

'Elsa isn't a beggar!'

'Not financially, or I shouldn't have suggested the match. But she's getting on, you know, and has no pretensions to brains or looks or anything of that sort.'

'You seem to forget that she's my daughter.'

'That shows my generosity. But, seriously, I don't see what there is against Wratislav. He has no debts – at least, nothing worth speaking about.'

'But think of his reputation! If half the things they say about him are true –'

'Probably three-quarters of them are. But what of it? You don't want an archangel for a son-in-law.'

'I don't want Wratislav. My poor Elsa would be miserable with him.'

'A little misery wouldn't matter very much with her; it would go so well with the way she does her hair, and if she couldn't get on with Wratislav she could always go and do good among the poor.'

The Baroness picked up a framed photograph from the table.

'He certainly is very handsome,' she said doubtfully; adding even more doubtfully, 'I dare say dear Elsa might reform him.'

The Gräfin had the presence of mind to laugh in the right key.

Three weeks later the Gräfin bore down upon the Baroness Sophie in a foreign bookseller's shop in the Graben, where she was, possibly, buying books of devotion, though it was the wrong counter for them.

'I've just left the dear children at the Rodenstahls',' was the Gräfin's greeting.

'Were they looking very happy?' asked the Baroness.

'Wratislav was wearing some new English clothes, so, of course, he was quite happy. I overheard him telling Toni a rather amusing story about a nun and a mousetrap, which won't bear repetition. Elsa was telling every one else a witticism about the Triple Alliance being like a paper umbrella – which seems to bear repetition with Christian fortitude.'

'Did they seem much wrapped up in each other?'

'To be candid, Elsa looked as if she were wrapped up in a horse-rug. And why let her wear saffron colour?'

'I always think it goes with her complexion.'

'Unfortunately it doesn't. It stays with it. Ugh. Don't forget, you're lunching with me on Thursday.'

The Baroness was late for her luncheon engagement the following Thursday.

'Imagine what has happened!' she screamed as she burst into the room.

'Something remarkable, to make you late for a meal,' said the Gräfin.

'Elsa has run away with the Rodenstahls' chauffeur!'

'Kolossal!'

'Such a thing as that no one in our family has ever done,' gasped the Baroness.

'Perhaps he didn't appeal to them in the same way,' suggested the Gräfin judicially.

The Baroness began to feel that she was not getting the astonishment and sympathy to which her catastrophe entitled her.

'At any rate,' she snapped, 'now she can't marry Wratislav.'

'She couldn't in any case,' said the Gräfin; 'he left suddenly for abroad last night.'

'For abroad! Where?'

'For Mexico, I believe.'

'Mexico! But what for? Why Mexico?'

'The English have a proverb, "Conscience makes cowboys of us all."'

'I didn't know Wratislav had a conscience.'

'My dear Sophie, he hasn't. It's other people's consciences that send one abroad in a hurry. Let's go and eat.'

The Easter Egg

It was distinctly hard lines for Lady Barbara, who came of good fighting stock, and was one of the bravest women of her generation, that her son should be so undisguisedly a coward. Whatever good qualities Lester Slaggby may have possessed, and he was in some respects charming, courage could certainly never be imputed to him. As a child he had suffered from childish timidity, as a boy from unboyish funk, and as a youth he had exchanged unreasoning fears for others which were more formidable from the fact of having a carefully-thought-out basis. He was frankly afraid of animals, nervous with firearms, and never crossed the Channel without mentally comparing the numerical proportion of life belts to passengers. On horseback he seemed to require as many hands as a Hindu god, at least four for clutching the reins, and two more for patting the horse soothingly on the neck. Lady Barbara no longer pretended not to see her son's prevailing weakness; with her usual courage she faced the knowledge of it squarely, and, mother-like, loved him none the less.

Continental travel, anywhere away from the great tourist tracks, was a favoured hobby with Lady Barbara, and Lester joined her as often as possible. Eastertide usually found her at Knobaltheim, an upland township in one of those small princedoms that make inconspicuous freckles on the map of Central Europe.

A long-standing acquaintanceship with the reigning family made her a personage of due importance in the eyes of her old friend the Burgomaster, and she was anxiously consulted by that worthy on the momentous occasion when the Prince made known his intention of coming in person to open a sanatorium outside the town. All the usual items in a programme of welcome, some of them fatuous and commonplace, others quaint and charming, had been arranged for, but the Burgomaster hoped that the resourceful English lady might have something new and tasteful to suggest in the way of loyal greeting. The Prince was known to the outside world, if at all, as an old-fashioned reactionary, combating modern progress, as it were, with a wooden sword; to his own people he was known as a kindly old gentleman with a certain endearing stateliness which had nothing of standoffishness about it. Knobaltheim was anxious to do its best. Lady Barbara discussed the matter with Lester and one or two acquaintances in her little hotel, but ideas were difficult to come by.

'Might I suggest something to the gnädige Frau?' asked a sallow high-cheek-boned lady to whom the

Englishwoman had spoken once or twice, and whom she had set down in her mind as probably a Southern Slav.

'Might I suggest something for the Reception Fest?' she went on, with a certain shy eagerness. 'Our little child here, our baby, we will dress him in little white coat, with small wings, as an Easter angel, and he will carry a large white Easter egg, and inside shall be a basket of plover eggs, of which the Prince is so fond, and he shall give it to his Highness as Easter offering. It is so pretty an idea; we have seen it done once in Styria.'

Lady Barbara looked dubiously at the proposed Easter angel, a fair, wooden-faced child of about four years old. She had noticed it the day before in the hotel, and wondered rather how such a towheaded child could belong to such a dark-visaged couple as the woman and her husband; probably, she thought, an adopted baby, especially as the couple were not young.

'Of course Gnädige Frau will escort the little child up to the Prince,' pursued the woman; 'but he will be quite good, and do as he is told.'

'We haf some pluffers' eggs shall come fresh from Wien,' said the husband.

The small child and Lady Barbara seemed equally unenthusiastic about the pretty idea; Lester was openly discouraging, but when the Burgomaster heard of it he was enchanted. The combination of sentiment and plovers' eggs appealed strongly to his Teutonic mind.

On the eventful day the Easter angel, really quite

prettily and quaintly dressed, was a centre of kindly interest to the gala crowd marshalled to receive his Highness.
The mother was unobtrusive and less fussy than most
parents would have been under the circumstances, merely
stipulating that she should place the Easter egg herself
in the arms that had been carefully schooled how to hold
the precious burden. Then Lady Barbara moved forward,
the child marching stolidly and with grim determination
at her side. It had been promised cakes and sweeties gal-
ore if it gave the egg well and truly to the kind old
gentleman who was waiting to receive it. Lester had tried
to convey to it privately that horrible smackings would
attend any failure in its share of the proceedings, but it
is doubtful if his German caused more than an immediate
distress. Lady Barbara had thoughtfully provided herself
with an emergency supply of chocolate sweetmeats; children may sometimes be timeservers, but they do not
encourage long accounts. As they approached nearer to
the princely dais Lady Barbara stood discreetly aside, and
the stolid-faced infant walked forward alone, with staggering but steadfast gait, encouraged by a murmur of
elderly approval. Lester, standing in the front row of the
onlookers, turned to scan the crowd for the beaming faces
of the happy parents. In a side-road which led to the railway station he saw a cab; entering the cab with every
appearance of furtive haste were the dark-visaged couple
who had been so plausibly eager for the 'pretty idea'. The
sharpened instinct of cowardice lit up the situation to

him in one swift flash. The blood roared and surged to his head as though thousands of floodgates had been opened in his veins and arteries, and his brain was the common sluice in which all the torrents met. He saw nothing but a blur around him. Then the blood ebbed away in quick waves, till his very heart seemed drained and empty, and he stood nervelessly, helplessly, dumbly watching the child, bearing its accursed burden with slow, relentless steps nearer and nearer to the group that waited sheep-like to receive him. A fascinated curiosity compelled Lester to turn his head towards the fugitives; the cab had started at hot pace in the direction of the station.

The next moment Lester was running, running faster than any of those present had ever seen a man run, and – he was not running away. For that stray fraction of his life some unwonted impulse beset him, some hint of the stock he came from, and he ran unflinchingly towards danger. He stooped and clutched at the Easter egg as one tries to scoop up the ball in Rugby football. What he meant to do with it he had not considered, the thing was to get it. But the child had been promised cakes and sweetmeats if it safely gave the egg into the hands of the kindly old gentleman; it uttered no scream, but it held to its charge with limpet grip. Lester sank to his knees, tugging savagely at the tightly clasped burden, and angry cries rose from the scandalized onlookers. A questioning, threatening ring formed round him, then shrank back in recoil as he shrieked out one hideous word. Lady Barbara heard the word and saw the crowd race away like scattered sheep, saw the Prince forcibly hustled away by his attendants; also she saw her son lying prone in an agony of overmastering terror, his spasm of daring shattered by the child's unexpected resistance, still clutching frantically, as though for safety, at that white-satin gew-gaw, unable to crawl even from its deadly neighbourhood, able only to scream and scream and scream. In her brain she was dimly conscious of balancing, or striving to balance, the abject shame which had him now in thrall against the one compelling act of courage which had flung him grandly and madly on to the point of danger. It was only for the fraction of a minute that she stood watching the two entangled figures, the infant with its woodenly obstinate face and body tense with dogged resistance, and the boy limp and already nearly dead with a terror that almost stifled his screams; and over them the long gala streamers flapping gaily in the sunshine. She never forgot the scene; but then, it was the last she ever saw.

Lady Barbara carries her scarred face with its sightless eyes as bravely as ever in the world, but at Eastertide her friends are careful to keep from her ears any mention of the children's Easter symbol.

Filboid Studge, the Story of a Mouse That Helped

'I want to marry your daughter,' said Mark Spayley with faltering eagerness. 'I am only an artist with an income of two hundred a year, and she is the daughter of an enormously wealthy man, so I suppose you will think my offer a piece of presumption.'

Duncan Dullamy, the great company inflator, showed no outward sign of displeasure. As a matter of fact, he was secretly relieved at the prospect of finding even a two-hundred-a-year husband for his daughter Leonore. A crisis was rapidly rushing upon him, from which he knew he would emerge with neither money nor credit; all his recent ventures had fallen flat, and flattest of all had gone the wonderful new breakfast food, Pipenta, on the advertisement of which he had sunk such huge sums. It could scarcely be called a drug in the market; people bought drugs, but no one bought Pipenta.

'Would you marry Leonore if she were a poor man's daughter?' asked the man of phantom wealth.

'Yes,' said Mark, wisely avoiding the error of over-protestation. And to his astonishment Leonore's father not only gave his consent, but suggested a fairly early date for the wedding.

'I wish I could show my gratitude in some way,' said Mark with genuine emotion. 'I'm afraid it's rather like the mouse proposing to help the lion.'

'Get people to buy that beastly muck,' said Dullamy, nodding savagely at a poster of the despised Pipenta, 'and you'll have done more than any of my agents have been able to accomplish.'

'It wants a better name,' said Mark reflectively, 'and something distinctive in the poster line. Anyway, I'll have a shot at it.'

Three weeks later the world was advised of the coming of a new breakfast food, heralded under the resounding name of 'Filboid Studge.' Spayley put forth no pictures of massive babies springing up with fungus-like rapidity under its forcing influence, or of representatives of the leading nations of the world scrambling with fatuous eagerness for its possession. One huge sombre poster depicted the Damned in Hell suffering a new torment from their inability to get at the Filboid Studge which elegant young fiends held in transparent bowls just beyond their reach. The scene was rendered even more gruesome by a subtle suggestion of the features of leading men and women of the day in the portrayal of the Lost Souls; prominent individuals of both political parties,

Society hostesses, well-known dramatic authors and novelists, and distinguished aeroplanists were dimly recognizable in that doomed throng; noted lights of the musical-comedy stage flickered wanly in the shades of the Inferno, smiling still from force of habit, but with the fearsome smiling rage of baffled effort. The poster bore no fulsome allusions to the merits of the new breakfast food, but a single grim statement ran in bold letters along its base: 'They cannot buy it now.'

Spayley had grasped the fact that people will do things from a sense of duty which they would never attempt as a pleasure. There are thousands of respectable middle-class men who, if you found them unexpectedly in a Turkish bath, would explain in all sincerity that a doctor had ordered them to take Turkish baths; if you told them in return that you went there because you liked it, they would stare in pained wonder at the frivolity of your motive. In the same way, whenever a massacre of Armenians is reported from Asia Minor, everyone assumes that it has been carried out 'under orders' from somewhere or another; no one seems to think that there are people who might *like* to kill their neighbours now and then.

And so it was with the new breakfast food. No one would have eaten Filboid Studge as a pleasure, but the grim austerity of its advertisement drove housewives in shoals to the grocers' shops to clamour for an immediate supply. In small kitchens solemn pigtailed daughters helped depressed mothers to perform the primitive ritual of its preparation. On the breakfast-tables of cheerless parlours it was partaken of in silence. Once the women-folk discovered that it was thoroughly unpalatable, their zeal in forcing it on their households knew no bounds. 'You haven't eaten your Filboid Studge!' would be screamed at the appetiteless clerk as he hurried wearily from the breakfast-table, and his evening meal would be prefaced by a warmed-up mess which would be explained as 'your Filboid Studge that you didn't eat this morning'. Those strange fanatics who ostentatiously mortify them-selves, inwardly and outwardly, with health biscuits and health garments, battened aggressively on the new food. Earnest spectacled young men devoured it on the steps of the National Liberal Club. A bishop who did not believe in a future state preached against the poster, and a peer's daughter died from eating too much of the com-pound. A further advertisement was obtained when an infantry regiment mutinied and shot its officers rather than eat the nauseous mess; fortunately, Lord Birrell of Blatherstone, who was War Minister at the moment, saved the situation by his happy epigram, that 'Discipline to be effective must be optional.'

Filboid Studge had become a household word, but Dullamy wisely realized that it was not necessarily the last word in breakfast dietary; its supremacy would be challenged as soon as some yet more unpalatable food should be put on the market. There might even be a reac-tion in favour of something tasty and appetizing, and the

Puritan austerity of the moment might be banished from domestic cookery. At an opportune moment, therefore, he sold out his interests in the article which had brought him in colossal wealth at a critical juncture, and placed his financial reputation beyond the reach of cavil. As for Leonore, who was now an heiress on a far greater scale than ever before, he naturally found her something a vast deal higher in the husband market than a two-hundred-a-year poster designer. Mark Spayley, the brainmouse who had helped the financial lion with such untoward effect, was left to curse the day he produced the wonder-working poster.

'After all,' said Clovis, meeting him shortly afterwards at his club, 'you have this doubtful consolation, that 'tis not in mortals to countermand success.'

The Music on the Hill

Sylvia Seltoun ate her breakfast in the morning-room at Yessney with a pleasant sense of ultimate victory, such as a fervent Ironside might have permitted himself on the morrow of Worcester fight. She was scarcely pugnacious by temperament, but belonged to that more successful class of fighters who are pugnacious by circumstance. Fate had willed that her life should be occupied with a series of small struggles, usually with the odds slightly against her, and usually she had just managed to come through winning. And now she felt that she had brought her hardest and certainly her most important struggle to a successful issue. To have married Mortimer Seltoun, 'Dead Mortimer' as his more intimate enemies called him, in the teeth of the cold hostility of his family, and in spite of his unaffected indifference to women, was indeed an achievement that had needed some determination and adroitness to carry through; yesterday she had brought her victory to its concluding stage by wrenching her husband away from Town and its group of satellite watering-places and 'settling him down', in the vocabu-lary of her kind, in this remote wood-girt manor farm which was his country house.

'You will never get Mortimer to go,' his mother had said carpingly, 'but if he once goes he'll stay; Yessney throws almost as much a spell over him as Town does. One can understand what holds him to Town, but Yessney –' and the dowager had shrugged her shoulders.

There was a sombre almost savage wildness about Yess-ney that was certainly not likely to appeal to town-bred tastes, and Sylvia, notwithstanding her name, was accus-tomed to nothing much more sylvan than 'leafy Kensington'. She looked on the country as something excellent and wholesome in its way, which was apt to become troublesome if you encouraged it overmuch. Dis-trust of town-life had been a new thing with her, born of her marriage with Mortimer, and she had watched with satisfaction the gradual fading of what she called 'the Jermyn-Street-look' in his eyes as the woods and heather of Yessney had closed in on them yesternight. Her will-power and strategy had prevailed; Mortimer would stay.

Outside the morning-room windows was a triangular slope of turf, which the indulgent might call a lawn, and beyond its low hedge of neglected fuschia bushes a steeper slope of heather and bracken dropped down into cavernous combes overgrown with oak and yew. In its wild open savagery there seemed a stealthy linking of the joy of life with the terror of unseen things. Sylvia smiled complacently as she gazed with a School-of-Art appreciation at the landscape, and then of a sudden she almost shuddered.

'It is very wild,' she said to Mortimer, who had joined her; 'one could almost think that in such a place the worship of Pan had never quite died out.'

'The worship of Pan never has died out,' said Mortimer. 'Other newer gods have drawn aside his votaries from time to time, but he is the Nature-God to whom all must come back at last. He has been called the Father of all the Gods, but most of his children have been stillborn.'

Sylvia was religious in an honest, vaguely devotional kind of way, and did not like to hear her beliefs spoken of as mere after-growths, but it was at least something new and hopeful to hear Dead Mortimer speak with such energy and conviction on any subject.

'You don't really believe in Pan?' she asked incredulously.

'I've been a fool in most things,' said Mortimer quietly, 'but I'm not such a fool as not to believe in Pan when I'm down here. And if you're wise you won't disbelieve in him too boastfully while you're in his country.'

It was not till a week later, when Sylvia had exhausted the attractions of the woodland walks round Yessney, that she ventured on a tour of inspection of the farm buildings. A farmyard suggested in her mind a scene of cheerful bustle, with churns and flails and smiling dairymaids, and teams of horses drinking knee-deep in duck-crowded ponds. As she wandered among the gaunt grey buildings of Yessney manor farm her first impression was one of crushing stillness and desolation, as though she had happened on some lone deserted homestead long given over to owls and cobwebs; then came a sense of furtive watchful hostility, the same shadow of unseen things that seemed to lurk in the wooded combes and coppices. From behind heavy doors and shuttered windows came the restless stamp of hoof or rasp of chain halter, and at times a muffled bellow from some stalled beast. From a distant corner a shaggy dog watched her with intent unfriendly eyes; as she drew near it slipped quietly into its kennel, and slipped out again as noiselessly when she had passed by. A few hens, questing for food under a rick, stole away under a gate at her approach. Sylvia felt that if she had come across any human beings in this wilderness of barn and byre they would have fled wraith-like from her gaze. At last, turning a corner quickly, she came upon a living thing that did not fly from her. Astretch in a pool of mud was an enormous sow, gigantic beyond the town-woman's wildest computation of swine-flesh, and speedily alert to resent and if necessary repel the unwonted intrusion. It was Sylvia's turn to make an unobtrusive retreat. As she threaded her way past rickyards and cowsheds and long blank walls, she started suddenly at a strange sound – the echo of a boy's laughter, golden and equivocal. Jan, the only boy employed on the farm, a tow-headed, wizen-faced yokel, was visibly at work on a potato clearing half-way up the nearest hill-side, and Mortimer, when questioned, knew of no other probable or possible begetter of the hidden mockery that had ambushed Sylvia's retreat. The memory of that untraceable echo was added to her other impressions of a furtive sinister 'something' that hung around Yessney.

Of Mortimer she saw very little; farm and woods and trout-streams seemed to swallow him up from dawn till dusk. Once, following the direction she had seen him take in the morning, she came to an open space in a nut copse, further shut in by huge yew trees, in the centre of which stood a stone pedestal surmounted by a small bronze figure of a youthful Pan. It was a beautiful piece of workmanship, but her attention was chiefly held by the fact that a newly cut bunch of grapes had been placed as an offering at its feet. Grapes were none too plentiful at the manor house, and Sylvia snatched the bunch angrily from the pedestal. Contemptuous annoyance dominated her thoughts as she strolled slowly homeward, and then gave way to a sharp feeling of something that was very near fright; across a thick tangle of undergrowth a boy's face was scowling at her, brown and beautiful, with unutterably evil eyes. It was a lonely pathway, all pathways round Yessney were lonely for the matter of that, and she sped forward without waiting to give a closer scrutiny to this sudden apparition. It was not till she had reached the house that she discovered that she had dropped the bunch of grapes in her flight.

'I saw a youth in the wood today,' she told Mortimer that evening, 'brown-faced and rather handsome, but a scoundrel to look at, A gipsy lad, I suppose.'

'A reasonable theory,' said Mortimer, 'only there aren't any gipsies in these parts at present.'

'Then who was he?' asked Sylvia, and as Mortimer appeared to have no theory of his own, she passed on to recount her finding of the votive offering.

'I suppose it was your doing,' she observed; 'it's a harmless piece of lunacy, but people would think you dreadfully silly if they knew of it.'

'Did you meddle with it in any way?' asked Mortimer.

'I – I threw the grapes away. It seemed so silly,' said Sylvia, watching Mortimer's impassive face for a sign of annoyance.

'I don't think you were wise to do that,' he said reflectively. 'I've heard it said that the Wood Gods are rather horrible to those who molest them.'

'Horrible perhaps to those that believe in them, but you see I don't,' retorted Sylvia.

'All the same,' said Mortimer in his even, dispassionate tone, 'I should avoid the woods and orchards if I were you, and give a wide berth to the horned beasts on the farm.'

It was all nonsense, of course, but in that lonely

wood-girt spot nonsense seemed able to rear a bastard brood of uneasiness.

'Mortimer,' said Sylvia suddenly, 'I think we will go back to Town some time soon.'

Her victory had not been so complete as she had supposed; it had carried her on to ground that she was already anxious to quit.

'I don't think you will ever go back to Town,' said Mortimer. He seemed to be paraphrasing his mother's prediction as to himself.

Sylvia noted with dissatisfaction and some self-contempt that the course of her next afternoon's ramble took her instinctively clear of the network of woods. As to the horned cattle, Mortimer's warning was scarcely needed, for she had always regarded them as of doubtful neutrality at the best: her imagination unsexed the most matronly dairy cows and turned them into bulls liable to 'see red' at any moment. The ram who fed in the narrow paddock below the orchards she had adjudged, after ample and cautious probation, to be of docile temper; today, however, she decided to leave his docility untested, for the usually tranquil beast was roaming with every sign of restlessness from corner to corner of his meadow. A low, fitful piping, as of some reedy flute, was coming from the depth of a neighbouring copse, and there seemed to be some subtle connection between the animal's restless pacing and the wild music from the wood. Sylvia turned her steps in an upward direction and climbed the heather-clad slopes that stretched in rolling shoulders high above Yessney. She had left the piping notes behind her, but across the wooded combes at her feet the wind brought her another kind of music, the straining bay of hounds in full chase. Yessney was just on the outskirts of the Devon-and-Somerset country, and the hunted deer sometimes came that way. Sylvia could presently see a dark body, breasting hill after hill, and sinking again and again out of sight as he crossed the combes, while behind him steadily swelled that relentless chorus, and she grew tense with the excited sympathy that one feels for any hunted thing in whose capture one is not directly interested. And at last he broke through the outermost line of oak scrub and fern and stood panting in the open, a fat September stag carrying a well-furnished head. His obvious course was to drop down to the brown pools of Undercombe, and thence make his way towards the red deer's favoured sanctuary, the sea. To Sylvia's surprise, however, he turned his head to the upland slope and came lumbering resolutely onward over the heather. 'It will be dreadful,' she thought, 'the hounds will pull him down under my very eyes.' But the music of the pack seemed to have died away for a moment, and in its place she heard again that wild piping, which rose now on this side, now on that, as though urging the failing stag to a final effort. Sylvia stood well aside from his path, half hidden in a thick growth of whortle bushes, and watched him swing stiffly upward, his flanks dark with sweat, the coarse hair on his neck showing light by contrast. The pipe music shrilled suddenly around her, seeming to come from the bushes at her very feet, and at the same moment the great beast slewed round and bore directly down upon her. In an instant her pity for the hunted animal was changed to wild terror at her own danger; the thick heather roots mocked her scrambling efforts at flight, and she looked frantically downward for a glimpse of oncoming hounds. The huge antler spikes were within a few yards of her, and in a flash of numbing fear she remembered Mortimer's warning, to beware of horned beasts on the farm. And then with a quick throb of joy she saw that she was not alone; a human figure stood a few paces aside, knee-deep in the whortle bushes.

'Drive it off!' she shrieked. But the figure made no answering movement.

The antlers drove straight at her breast, the acrid smell of the hunted animal was in her nostrils, but her eyes were filled with the horror of something she saw other than her oncoming death. And in her ears rang the echo of a boy's laughter, golden and equivocal.

The Story of St Vespaluus

'Tell me a story,' said the Baroness, staring out despairingly at the rain; it was that light, apologetic sort of rain that looks as if it was going to leave off every minute and goes on for the greater part of the afternoon.

'What sort of story?' asked Clovis, giving his croquet mallet a valedictory shove into retirement.

'One just true enough to be interesting and not true enough to be tiresome,' said the Baroness.

Clovis rearranged several cushions to his personal solace and satisfaction; he knew that the Baroness liked her guests to be comfortable, and he thought it right to respect her wishes in that particular.

'Have I ever told you the story of St Vespaluus?' he asked.

'You've told me stories about grand-dukes and lion-tamers and financiers' widows and a postmaster in Herzegovina,' said the Baroness, 'and about an Italian jockey and an amateur governess who went to Warsaw, and several about your mother, but certainly never anything about a saint.'

'This story happened a long while ago,' he said, 'in those uncomfortable piebald times when a third of the people were Pagan, and a third Christian, and the biggest third of all just followed whichever religion the Court happened to profess. There was a certain king called Hkrikros, who had a fearful temper and no immediate successor in his own family; his married sister, however, had provided him with a large stock of nephews from which to select his heir. And the most eligible and royally-approved of all these nephews was the sixteen-year-old Vespaluus. He was the best looking, and the best horseman and javelin-thrower, and had that priceless princely gift of being able to walk past a supplicant with an air of not having seen him, but would certainly have given something if he had. My mother has that gift to a certain extent; she can go smilingly and financially unscathed through a charity bazaar, and meet the organizers next day with a solicitous "had I but known you were in need of funds" air that is really rather a triumph in audacity. Now Hkrikros was a Pagan of the first water, and kept the worship of the sacred serpents, who lived in a hallowed grove on a hill near the royal palace, up to a high pitch of enthusiasm. The common people were allowed to please themselves, within certain discreet limits, in the matter of private religion, but any official in the service of the Court who went over to the new cult was looked down on, literally as well as metaphorically, the looking down being done from the gallery that ran round the royal bear-pit. Consequently there was considerable scandal and consternation when the youthful Vespaluus appeared one day at a Court function with a rosary tucked into his belt, and announced in reply to angry questionings that he had decided to adopt Christianity, or at any rate to give it a trial. If it had been any of the other nephews the king would possibly have ordered something drastic in the way of scourging and banishment, but in the case of the favoured Vespaluus he determined to look on the whole thing much as a modern father might regard the announced intention of his son to adopt the stage as a profession. He sent accordingly for the Royal Librarian. The royal library in those days was not a very extensive affair, and the keeper of the king's books had a great deal of leisure on his hands. Consequently he was in frequent demand for the settlement of other people's affairs when these strayed beyond normal limits and got temporarily unmanageable.

'"You must reason with Prince Vespaluus," said the king, "and impress on him the error of his ways. We cannot have the heir to the throne setting such a dangerous example."

'"But where shall I find the necessary arguments?" asked the Librarian.

'"I give you free leave to pick and choose your arguments in the royal woods and coppices," said the king; "if you cannot get together some cutting observations

119

and stinging retorts suitable to the occasion you are a person of very poor resource."

'So the Librarian went into the woods and gathered a goodly selection of highly argumentative rods and switches, and then proceeded to reason with Vespaluus on the folly and iniquity and above all the unseemliness of his conduct. His reasoning left a deep impression on the young prince, an impression which lasted for many weeks, during which time nothing more was heard about the unfortunate lapse into Christianity. Then a further scandal of the same nature agitated the Court. At a time when he should have been engaged in audibly invoking the gracious protection and patronage of the holy serpents, Vespaluus was heard singing a chant in honour of St Odilo of Cluny. The king was furious at this new outbreak, and began to take a gloomy view of the situation; Vespaluus was evidently going to show a dangerous obstinacy in persisting in his heresy. And yet there was nothing in his appearance to justify such perverseness; he had not the pale eye of the fanatic or the mystic look of the dreamer. On the contrary, he was quite the best-looking boy at Court; he had an elegant, well-knit figure, a healthy complexion, eyes the colour of very ripe mulberries, and dark hair, smooth and very well cared for.'

'It sounds like a description of what you imagine yourself to have been like at the age of sixteen,' said the Baroness.

'My mother has probably been showing you some of

my early photographs,' said Clovis. Having turned the sarcasm into a compliment, he resumed his story.

'The king had Vespaluus shut up in a dark tower for three days, with nothing but bread and water to live on, the squealing and fluttering of bats to listen to, and drifting clouds to watch through one little window slit. The anti-Pagan section of the community began to talk portentously of the boy-martyr. The martyrdom was mitigated, as far as the food was concerned, by the carelessness of the tower warden, who once or twice left a portion of his own supper of broiled meat and fruit and wine by mistake in the prince's cell. After the punishment was over, Vespaluus was closely watched for any further symptom of religious perversity, for the king was determined to stand no more opposition on so important a matter, even from a favourite nephew. If there was any more of this nonsense, he said, the succession to the throne would have to be altered.

'For a time all went well; the festival of summer sports was approaching, and the young Vespaluus was too engrossed in wrestling and foot-running and javelin-throwing competitions to bother himself with the strife of conflicting religious systems. Then, however, came the great culminating feature of the summer festival, the ceremonial dance round the grove of the sacred serpents, and Vespaluus, as we should say, "sat it out". The affront to the State religion was too public and ostentatious to be overlooked, even if the king had been so minded, and he was not in the least so minded. For a day and a half he sat apart and brooded, and every one thought he was debating within himself the question of the young prince's death or pardon; as a matter of fact he was merely thinking out the manner of the boy's death. As the thing had to be done, and was bound to attract an enormous amount of public attention in any case, it was as well to make it as spectacular and impressive as possible.

'"Apart from his unfortunate taste in religions," said the king, "and his obstinacy in adhering to it, he is a sweet and pleasant youth, therefore it is meet and fitting that he should be done to death by the winged envoys of sweetness."

'"Your Majesty means – ?" said the Royal Librarian.

'"I mean," said the king, "that he shall be stung to death by bees. By the royal bees, of course."

'"A most elegant death," said the Librarian.

'"Elegant and spectacular, and decidedly painful," said the king; "it fulfills all the conditions that could be wished for."

'The king himself thought out all the details of the execution ceremony. Vespaluus was to be stripped of his clothes, his hands were to be bound behind him, and he was then to be slung in a recumbent position immediately above three of the largest of the royal beehives, so that the least movement of his body would bring him in jarring contact with them. The rest could be safely left to the bees. The death throes, the king computed, might last anything from fifteen to forty minutes, though there was division of opinion and considerable wagering among the other nephews as to whether death might not be almost instantaneous, or, on the other hand, whether it might not be deferred for a couple of hours. Anyway, they all agreed, it was vastly preferable to being thrown down into an evil smelling bear-pit and being clawed and mauled to death by imperfectly carnivorous animals.

'It so happened, however, that the keeper of the royal hives had leanings towards Christianity himself, and moreover, like most of the Court officials, he was very much attached to Vespaluus. On the eve of the execution, therefore, he busied himself with removing the stings from all the royal bees; it was a long and delicate operation, but he was an expert beemaster, and by working hard nearly all night he succeeded in disarming all, or almost all, of the hive inmates.'

'I didn't know you could take the sting from a live bee,' said the Baroness incredulously.

'Every profession has its secrets,' replied Clovis; 'if it hadn't it wouldn't be a profession. Well, the moment for the execution arrived; the king and Court took their places, and accommodation was found for as many of the populace as wished to witness the unusual spectacle. Fortunately the royal bee-yard was of considerable dimensions, and was commanded, moreover, by the terraces that ran round the royal gardens; with a little squeezing and the erection of a few platforms room was found for everybody. Vespaluus was carried into the open space in front of the hives, blushing and slightly embarrassed, but not at all displeased at the attention which was being centred on him.'

'He seems to have resembled you in more things than in appearance,' said the Baroness.

'Don't interrupt at a critical point in the story,' said Clovis. 'As soon as he had been carefully adjusted in the prescribed position over the hives, and almost before the gaolers had time to retire to a safe distance, Vespaluus gave a lusty and well-aimed kick, which sent all three hives toppling one over another. The next moment he was wrapped from head to foot in bees; each individual insect nursed the dreadful and humiliating knowledge that in this supreme hour of catastrophe it could not sting, but each felt that it ought to pretend to. Vespaluus squealed and wriggled with laughter, for he was being tickled nearly to death, and now and again he gave a furious kick and used a bad word as one of the few bees that had escaped disarmament got its protest home. But the spectators saw with amazement that he showed no signs of approaching death agony, and as the bees dropped wearily away in clusters from his body his flesh was seen to be as white and smooth as before the ordeal, with a shiny glaze from the honey-smear of innumerable bee-feet, and here and there a small red spot where one of the rare stings had left its mark. It was obvious that a miracle had been performed in his favour, and one loud murmur, of astonishment or exultation, rose from the onlooking crowd. The king gave orders for Vespaluus to be taken down to await further orders, and stalked silently back to his midday meal, at which he was careful to eat heartily and drink copiously as though nothing unusual had happened. After dinner he sent for the Royal Librarian.

' "What is the meaning of this fiasco?" he demanded.

' "Your Majesty," said that official, "either there is something radically wrong with the bees –"

' "There is nothing wrong with my bees," said the king haughtily, "they are the best bees."

' "Or else," said the Librarian, "there is something irremediably right about Prince Vespaluus."

' "If Vespaluus is right I must be wrong," said the king.

'The Librarian was silent for a moment. Hasty speech has been the downfall of many; ill-considered silence was the undoing of the luckless Court functionary.

'Forgetting the restraint due to his dignity, and the golden rule which imposes repose of mind and body after a heavy meal, the king rushed upon the keeper of the royal books and hit him repeatedly and promiscuously over the head with an ivory chessboard, a pewter wine-flagon, and a brass candlestick; he knocked him violently and often against an iron torch sconce, and kicked him thrice round the banqueting chamber with rapid, energetic kicks. Finally, he dragged him down a long passage by the hair of his head and flung him out of a window into the courtyard below.'

'Was he much hurt?' asked the Baroness.

'More hurt than surprised,' said Clovis. 'You see, the king was notorious for his violent temper. However, this was the first time he had let himself go so unrestrainedly on the top of a heavy meal. The Librarian lingered for many days – in fact, for all I know, he may have ultimately recovered, but Hkrikros died that same evening. Vespaluus had hardly finished getting the honey stains off his body before a hurried deputation came to put the coronation oil on his head. And what with the publicly-witnessed miracle and the accession of a Christian sovereign, it was not surprising that there was a general scramble of converts to the new religion. A hastily consecrated bishop was overworked with a rush of baptisms in the hastily improvised Cathedral of St Odilo. And the boy-martyr-that-might-have-been was transposed in the popular imagination into a royal boy-saint, whose fame attracted throngs of curious and devout sightseers to the capital. Vespaluus, who was busily engaged in organizing the games and athletic contests that were to mark the commencement of his reign, had no time to give heed to the religious fervour which was effervescing round his personality; the first indication he had of the existing state of affairs was when the Court Chamberlain (a recent and very ardent addition to the Christian community) brought for his approval the outlines of a projected ceremonial cutting-down of the idolatrous serpent-grove.

' "Your Majesty will be graciously pleased to cut down

the first tree with a specially consecrated axe," said the obsequious official.

' "I'll cut off your head first, with any axe that comes handy," said Vespaluus indignantly; "do you suppose that I'm going to begin my reign by mortally affronting the sacred serpents? It would be most unlucky."

' "But your Majesty's Christian principles?" exclaimed the bewildered Chamberlain.

' "I never had any," said Vespaluus; "I used to pretend to be a Christian convert just to annoy Hkrikros. He used to fly into such delicious tempers. And it was rather fun being whipped and scolded and shut up in a tower all for nothing. But as to turning Christian in real earnest, like you people seem to do, I couldn't think of such a thing. And the holy and esteemed serpents have always helped me when I've prayed to them for success in my running and wrestling and hunting, and it was through their distinguished intercession that the bees were not able to hurt me with their stings. It would be black ingratitude to turn against their worship at the very outset of my reign. I hate you for suggesting it."

'The Chamberlain wrung his hands despairingly.

' "But, your Majesty," he wailed, "the people are reverencing you as a saint, and the nobles are being Christianized in batches, and neighbouring potentates of that Faith are sending special envoys to welcome you as a brother. There is some talk of making you the patron saint of beehives, and a certain shade of honey-yellow has been christened Vespalussian gold at the Emperor's Court. You can't surely go back on all this."

'"I don't mind being reverenced and greeted and honoured," said Vespaluus; "I don't even mind being sainted in moderation, as long as I'm not expected to be saintly as well. But I wish you clearly and finally to understand that I will *not* give up the worship of the august and auspicious serpents."

'There was a world of unspoken bear-pit in the way he uttered those last words, and the mulberry-dark eyes flashed dangerously.

'"A new reign," said the Chamberlain to himself, "but the same old temper."

'Finally, as a State necessity, the matter of the religions was compromised. At stated intervals the king appeared before his subjects in the national cathedral in the character of St Vespaluus, and the idolatrous grove was gradually pruned and lopped away till nothing remained of it. But the sacred and esteemed serpents were removed to a private shrubbery in the royal gardens, where Vespaluus the Pagan and certain members of his household devoutly and decently worshipped them. That possibly is the reason why the boy-king's success in sports and hunting never deserted him to the end of his days, and that is also the reason why, in spite of the popular veneration for his sanctity, he never received official canonization.'

'It has stopped raining,' said the Baroness.

The Way to the Dairy

The Baroness and Clovis sat in a much-frequented corner of the Park exchanging biographical confidences about the long succession of passers-by.

'Who are those depressed-looking young women who have just gone by?' asked the Baroness; 'they have the air of people who have bowed to destiny and are not quite sure whether the salute will be returned.'

'Those,' said Clovis, 'are the Brimley Bomefields. I dare say you would look depressed if you had been through their experiences.'

'I'm always having depressing experiences,' said the Baroness, 'but I never give them outward expression. It's as bad as looking one's age. Tell me about the Brimley Bomefields.'

'Well,' said Clovis, 'the beginning of their tragedy was that they found an aunt. The aunt had been there all the time, but they had very nearly forgotten her existence until a distant relative refreshed their memory by remembering her very distinctly in his will; it is wonderful what the force of example will accomplish. The aunt, who had been unobtrusively poor, became quite pleasantly rich, and the Brimley Bomefields grew suddenly concerned at the loneliness of her life and took her under their collective wings. She had as many wings around her at this time as one of those beast-things in Revelation.'

'So far I don't see any tragedy from the Brimley Bomefields' point of view,' said the Baroness.

'We haven't got to it yet,' said Clovis. 'The aunt had been used to living very simply, and had seen next to nothing of what we should consider life, and her nieces didn't encourage her to do much in the way of making a splash with her money. Quite a good deal of it would come to them at her death, and she was a fairly old woman, but there was one circumstance which cast a shadow of gloom over the satisfaction they felt in the discovery and acquisition of this desirable aunt: she openly acknowledged that a comfortable slice of her little fortune would go to a nephew on the other side of her family. He was rather a deplorable thing in rotters, and quite hopelessly top-hole in the way of getting through money, but he had been more or less decent to the old lady in her unremembered days, and she wouldn't hear anything against him. At least, she wouldn't pay any attention to what she did hear, but her nieces took care that she should have to listen to a good deal in that line. It seemed such a pity, they said among themselves, that good money should fall into such worthless hands. They habitually spoke of their aunt's money as "good money", as though other people's aunts dabbled for the most part in spurious currency.

'Regularly after the Derby, St Leger, and other notable racing events they indulged in audible speculations as to how much money Roger had squandered in unfortunate betting transactions.

'"His travelling expenses must come to a big sum," said the eldest Brimley Bomefield one day; "they say he attends every race-meeting in England, besides others abroad. I shouldn't wonder if he went all the way to India to see the race for the Calcutta Sweepstake that one hears so much about."

'"Travel enlarges the mind, my dear Christine," said her aunt.

'"Yes, dear aunt, travel undertaken in the right spirit," agreed Christine; "but travel pursued merely as a means towards gambling and extravagant living is more likely to contract the purse than to enlarge the mind. However, as long as Roger enjoys himself, I suppose he doesn't care how fast or unprofitably the money goes, or where he is to find more. It seems a pity, that's all."

'The aunt by that time had begun to talk of something else, and it was doubtful if Christine's moralizing had been even accorded a hearing. It was her remark, however – the aunt's remark, I mean – about travel enlarging the mind, that gave the youngest Brimley Bomefield her great idea for the showing-up of Roger.

'"If aunt could only be taken somewhere to see him gambling and throwing away money," she said, "it would open her eyes to his character more effectually than anything we can say."

'"My dear Veronique," said her sisters, "we can't go following him to race-meetings."

'"Certainly not to race-meetings," said Veronique, "but we might go to some place where one can look on at gambling without taking part in it."

'"Do you mean Monte Carlo?" they asked her, beginning to jump rather at the idea.

'"Monte Carlo is a long way off, and has a dreadful reputation," said Veronique; "I shouldn't like to tell our friends that we were going to Monte Carlo. But I believe Roger usually goes to Dieppe about this time of year, and some quite respectable English people go there, and the journey wouldn't be expensive. If aunt could stand the Channel crossing the change of scene might do her a lot of good."

'And that was how the fateful idea came to the Brimley Bomefields.

'From the very first set-off disaster hung over the expedition, as they afterwards remembered. To begin with, all the Brimley Bomefields were extremely unwell during the crossing, while the aunt enjoyed the sea air and made friends with all manner of strange travelling companions. Then, although it was many years since she had been on the Continent, she had served a very practical apprenticeship there as a paid companion, and her knowledge of colloquial French beat theirs to a standstill. It became increasingly difficult to keep under their collective wings a person who knew what she wanted and was able to ask for it and to see that she got it. Also, as far as Roger was concerned, they drew Dieppe blank; it turned out that he was staying at Pourville, a little watering-place a mile or two further west. The Brimley Bomefields discovered that Dieppe was too crowded and frivolous, and persuaded the old lady to migrate to the comparative seclusion of Pourville.

' "You won't find it dull, you know," they assured her; "there is a little casino attached to the hotel, and you can watch the people dancing and throwing away their money at *petits chevaux*."

'It was just before *petits chevaux* had been supplanted by *boule*.

'Roger was not staying in the same hotel, but they knew that the casino would be certain of his patronage on most afternoons and evenings.

'On the first evening of their visit they wandered into the casino after a fairly early dinner, and hovered near the tables. Bertie van Tahn was staying there at the time, and he described the whole incident to me. The Brimley Bomefields kept a furtive watch on the doors as though they were expecting some one to turn up, and the aunt got more and more amused and interested watching the little horses whirl round and round the board.

' "Do you know, poor little number eight hasn't won for the last thirty-two times," she said to Christine; "I've been keeping count. I shall really have to put five francs on him to encourage him."

' "Come and watch the dancing, dear," said Christine nervously. It was scarcely a part of their strategy that Roger should come in and find the old lady backing her fancy at the *petits chevaux* table.

' "Just wait while I put five francs on number eight," said the aunt, and in another moment her money was lying on the table. The horses commenced to move round; it was a slow race this time, and number eight crept up at the finish like some crafty demon and placed his nose just a fraction in front of number three, who had seemed to be winning easily. Recourse had to be had to measurement, and the number eight was proclaimed the winner. The aunt picked up thirty-five francs. After that the Brimley Bomefields would have had to have used concerted force to get her away from the tables. When Roger appeared on the scene she was fifty-two francs to the good; her nieces were hovering forlornly in the background, like chickens that have been hatched out by a duck and are despairingly watching their parent disporting herself in a dangerous and uncongenial element. The supper-party which Roger insisted on standing that night in honour of his aunt and the three Miss Brimley Bomefields was remarkable for the unrestrained gaiety of two of the participants and the funereal mirthlessness of the remaining guests.

'"I do not think," Christine confided afterwards to a friend, who re-confided it to Bertie van Tahn, "that I shall ever be able to touch *pâté de foie gras* again. It would bring back memories of that awful evening."

'For the next two or three days the nieces made plans for returning to England or moving on to some other resort where there was no casino. The aunt was busy making a system for winning at *petits chevaux*. Number eight, her first love, had been running rather unkindly for her, and a series of plunges on number five had turned out even worse.

'"Do you know, I dropped over seven hundred francs at the tables this afternoon," she announced cheerfully at dinner on the fourth evening of their visit.

'"Aunt! Twenty-eight pounds! And you were losing last night too."

'"Oh, I shall get it all back," she said optimistically; "but not here. These silly little horses are no good. I shall go somewhere where one can play comfortably at roulette. You needn't look so shocked. I've always felt that, given the opportunity, I should be an inveterate gambler, and now you darlings have put the opportunity in my way. I must drink your very good healths. Waiter, a bottle of *Pontet Canet*. Ah, it's number seven on the wine list; I shall plunge on number seven tonight. It won four times running this afternoon when I was backing that silly number five."

'Number seven was not in a winning mood that evening. The Brimley Bomefields, tired of watching disaster from a distance, drew near to the table where their aunt was now an honoured habituée, and gazed mournfully at the successive victories of one and five and eight and four, which swept "good money" out of the purse of seven's obstinate backer. The day's losses totalled something very near two thousand francs.

' "You incorrigible gamblers," said Roger chaffingly to them, when he found them at the tables.

' "We are not gambling," said Christine freezingly; "we are looking on."

' "I *don't* think," said Roger knowingly; "of course you're a syndicate and aunt is putting the stakes on for all of you. Any one can tell by your looks when the wrong horse wins that you've got a stake on."

'Aunt and nephew had supper alone that night, or at least they would have if Bertie hadn't joined them; all the Brimley Bomefields had headaches.

'The aunt carried them all off to Dieppe the next day and set cheerily about the task of winning back some of her losses. Her luck was variable; in fact, she had some fair streaks of good fortune, just enough to keep her thoroughly amused with her new distraction; but on the whole she was a loser. The Brimley Bomefields had a collective attack of nervous prostration on the day when she sold out a quantity of shares in Argentine rails. "Nothing will ever bring that money back," they remarked lugubriously to one another.

'Veronique at last could bear it no longer, and went home; you see, it had been her idea to bring the aunt on this disastrous expedition, and though the others did not cast the fact verbally in her face, there was a certain lurking reproach in their eyes which was harder to meet than actual upbraidings. The other two remained behind, forlornly mounting guard over their aunt until such time as the waning of the Dieppe season should at last turn her in the direction of home and safety. They made anxious calculations as to how little "good money" might, with reasonable luck, be squandered in the meantime. Here, however, their reckoning went far astray; the close of the Dieppe season merely turned their aunt's thoughts in search of some other convenient gambling resort. "Show a cat the way to the dairy –" I forget how the proverb goes on, but it summed up the situation as far as the Brimley Bomefields' aunt was concerned. She had been introduced to unexplored pleasures, and found them greatly to her liking, and she was in no hurry to forgo the fruits of her newly acquired knowledge. You see, for the first time in her life the old thing was thoroughly enjoying herself; she was losing money, but she had plenty of fun and excitement over the process, and she had enough left to do very comfortably on. Indeed, she was only just learning to understand the art of doing oneself well. She was a popular hostess, and in return her fellow-gamblers were always ready to entertain her to dinners and suppers when their luck was in. Her nieces, who still remained in attendance on her, with the pathetic unwillingness of a crew to leave a foundering treasure ship which might yet be steered into port, found little pleasure in these Bohemian festivities; to see "good money" lavished on good living for the entertainment of a nondescript circle of acquaintances who were not likely to be in any way socially useful to them, did not attune them to a spirit of revelry. They contrived, whenever possible, to excuse themselves from participation in their aunt's deplored gaieties; the Brimley Bomefield headaches became famous.

'And one day the nieces came to the conclusion that, as they would have expressed it, "no useful purpose would be served" by their continued attendance on a relative who had so thoroughly emancipated herself from the sheltering protection of their wings. The aunt bore the announcement of their departure with a cheerfulness that was almost disconcerting.

' "It's time you went home and had those headaches seen to by a specialist," was her comment on the situation.

'The homeward journey of the Brimley Bomefields was a veritable retreat from Moscow, and what made it the more bitter was the fact that the Moscow, in this case, was not overwhelmed with fire and ashes, but merely extravagantly over-illuminated.

'From mutual friends and acquaintances they sometimes get glimpses of their prodigal relative, who has settled down into a confirmed gambling maniac, living on such salvage of income as obliging moneylenders have left at her disposal.

'So you need not be surprised,' concluded Clovis, 'if they do wear a depressed look in public.'

'Which is Veronique?' asked the Baroness.

'The most depressed-looking of the three,' said Clovis.

The Peace of Mowsle Barton

Crefton Lockyer sat at his ease, an ease alike of body and soul, in the little patch of ground, half-orchard and half-garden, that abutted on the farmyard at Mowsle Barton. After the stress and noise of long years of city life, the repose and peace of the hill-begirt homestead struck on his senses with an almost dramatic intensity. Time and space seemed to lose their meaning and their abruptness; the minutes slid away into hours, and the meadows and fallows sloped away into middle distance, softly and imperceptibly. Wild weeds of the hedgerow straggled into the flower-garden, and wallflowers and garden bushes made counter-raids into farmyard and lane. Sleepy-looking hens and solemn preoccupied ducks were equally at home in yard, orchard, or roadway; nothing seemed to belong definitely to anywhere; even the gates were not necessarily to be found on their hinges. And over the whole scene brooded the sense of a peace that had almost a quality of magic in it. In the afternoon you felt that it had always been afternoon, and must always remain afternoon; in the twilight you knew that it could never have been anything else but twilight. Crefton Lockyer sat at his ease in the rustic seat beneath an old medlar tree, and decided that here was the life-anchorage that his mind had so fondly pictured and that latterly his tired and jarred senses had so often pined for. He would make a permanent lodging-place among these simple friendly people, gradually increasing the modest comforts with which he would like to surround himself, but falling in as much as possible with their manner of living.

As he slowly matured this resolution in his mind an elderly woman came hobbling with uncertain gait through the orchard. He recognized her as a member of the farm household, the mother or possibly the mother-in-law of Mrs Spurfield, his present landlady, and hastily formulated some pleasant remark to make to her. She forestalled him.

'There's a bit of writing chalked up on the door over yonder. What is it?'

She spoke in a dull impersonal manner, as though the question had been on her lips for years and had best be got rid of. Her eyes, however, looked impatiently over Crefton's head at the door of a small barn which formed the outpost of a straggling line of farm buildings.

'Martha Pillamon is an old witch' was the announcement that met Crefton's inquiring scrutiny, and he hesitated a moment before giving the statement wider publicity. For all he knew to the contrary, it might be Martha herself to whom he was speaking. It was possible that Mrs Spurfield's maiden name had been Pillamon. And the gaunt, withered old dame at his side might certainly fulfil local conditions as to the outward aspect of a witch.

'It's something about someone called Martha Pilla-mon,' he explained cautiously.

'What does it say?'

'It's very disrespectful,' said Crefton; 'it says she's a witch. Such things ought not to be written up.'

'It's true, every word of it,' said his listener with considerable satisfaction, adding as a special descriptive note of her own, 'the old toad'.

And as she hobbled away through the farmyard she shrilled out in her cracked voice, 'Martha Pillamon is an old witch!'

'Did you hear what she said?' mumbled a weak, angry voice somewhere behind Crefton's shoulder. Turning hastily, he beheld another old crone, thin and yellow and wrinkled, and evidently in a high state of displeasure. Obviously this was Martha Pillamon in person. The orchard seemed to be a favourite promenade for the aged women of the neighbourhood.

' 'Tis lies, 'tis sinful lies,' the weak voice went on ' 'Tis Betsy Croot is the old witch. She an' her daughter, the dirty rat. I'll put a spell on 'em, the old nuisances.'

As she limped slowly away her eye caught the chalk inscription on the barn door.

'What's written up there?' she demanded, wheeling round on Crefton.

'Vote for Soarker,' he responded, with the craven boldness of the practised peacemaker.

The old woman grunted, and her mutterings and her faded red shawl lost themselves gradually among the tree-trunks. Crefton rose presently and made his way towards the farmhouse. Somehow a good deal of the peace seemed to have slipped out of the atmosphere.

The cheery bustle of tea-time in the old farm kitchen, which Crefton had found so agreeable on previous afternoons, seemed to have soured today into a certain uneasy melancholy. There was a dull, dragging silence around the board, and the tea itself, when Crefton came to taste it, was a flat, lukewarm concoction that would have driven the spirit of revelry out of a carnival.

'It's no use complaining of the tea,' said Mrs Spurfield hastily, as her guest stared with an air of polite inquiry at his cup. 'The kettle won't boil, that's the truth of it.'

Crefton turned to the hearth, where an unusually fierce fire was banked up under a big black kettle, which sent a thin wreath of steam from its spout, but seemed otherwise to ignore the action of the roaring blaze beneath it.

'It's been there more than an hour, an boil it won't,' said Mrs Spurfield, adding, by way of complete explanation, 'we're bewitched.'

'It's Martha Pillamon as has done it,' chimed in the

old mother; 'I'll be even with the old toad. I'll put a spell on her.'

'It must boil in time,' protested Crefton, ignoring the suggestions of foul influences. 'Perhaps the coal is damp.'

'It won't boil in time for supper, nor for breakfast tomorrow morning, not if you was to keep the fire a-going all night for it,' said Mrs Spurfield. And it didn't. The household subsisted on fried and baked dishes, and a neighbour obligingly brewed tea and sent it across in a moderately warm condition.

'I suppose you'll be leaving us now that things has turned up uncomfortable,' Mrs Spurfield observed at breakfast; 'there are folks as deserts one as soon as trouble comes.'

Crefton hurriedly disclaimed any immediate change of plans; he observed, however, to himself that the earlier heartiness of manner had in a large measure deserted the household. Suspicious looks, sulky silences, or sharp speeches had become the order of the day. As for the old mother, she sat about the kitchen or the garden all day, murmuring threats and spells against Martha Pillamon. There was something alike terrifying and piteous in the spectacle of these frail old morsels of humanity consecrating their last flickering energies to the task of making each other wretched. Hatred seemed to be the one faculty which had survived in undiminished vigour and intensity where all else was dropping into ordered and symmetrical decay. And the uncanny part of it was that some horrid unwholesome power seemed to be distilled from their spite and their cursings. No amount of sceptical explanation could remove the undoubted fact that neither kettle nor saucepan would come to boiling-point over the hottest fire. Crefton clung as long as possible to the theory of some defect in the coals, but a wood fire gave the same result, and when a small spirit-lamp kettle, which he ordered out by carrier, showed the same obstinate refusal to allow its contents to boil he felt that he had come suddenly into contact with some unguessed-at and very evil aspect of hidden forces. Miles away, down through an opening in the hills, he could catch glimpses of a road where motor-cars sometimes passed, and yet here, so little removed from the arteries of the latest civilization, was a bat-haunted old homestead, where something unmistakably like witchcraft seemed to hold a very practical sway.

Passing out through the farm garden on his way to the lanes beyond, where he hoped to recapture the comfortable sense of peacefulness that was so lacking around house and hearth – especially hearth – Crefton came across the old mother, sitting mumbling to herself in the seat beneath the medlar tree. 'Let un sink as swims, let un sink as swims,' she was repeating over and over again, as a child repeats a half-learned lesson. And now and then she would break off into a shrill laugh, with a note of malice in it that was not pleasant to hear. Crefton was glad when he found himself out of earshot, in the quiet and seclusion of the deep overgrown lanes that seemed to lead away to nowhere; one, narrower and deeper than the rest, attracted his footsteps, and he was almost annoyed when he found that it really did act as a miniature roadway to a human dwelling. A forlorn-looking cottage with a scrap of ill-tended cabbage garden and a few aged apple trees stood at an angle where a swift-flowing stream widened out for a space into a decent-sized pond before hurrying away again through the willows that had checked its course. Crefton leaned against a tree-trunk and looked across the swirling eddies of the pond at the humble little homestead opposite him; the only sign of life came from a small procession of dingy-looking ducks that marched in single file down to the water's edge. There is always something rather taking in the way a duck changes itself in an instant from a slow, clumsy waddler of the earth to a graceful, buoyant swimmer of the waters, and Crefton waited with a certain arrested attention to watch the leader of the file launch itself on to the surface of the pond. He was aware at the same time of a curious warning instinct that something strange and unpleasant was about to happen. The duck flung itself confidently forward into the water, and rolled immediately under the surface. Its head appeared for a moment and went under again, leaving a train of bubbles in its wake, while wings and legs churned the water in a helpless swirl of flapping and kicking. The bird was obviously drowning. Crefton thought at first that it had caught itself in some weeds, or was being attacked from below by a pike or water-rat. But no blood floated to the surface, and the wildly bobbing body made the circuit of the pond current without hindrance from any entanglement. A second duck had by this time launched itself into the pond, and a second struggling body rolled and twisted under the surface. There was something peculiarly piteous in the sight of the gasping beaks that showed now and again above the water, as though in terrified protest at this treachery of a trusted and familiar element. Crefton gazed with something like horror as a third duck poised itself on the bank and splashed in, to share the fate of the other two. He felt almost relieved when the remainder of the flock, taking tardy alarm from the commotion of the slowly drowning bodies, drew themselves up with tense outstretched necks, and sidled away from the scene of danger, quacking a deep note of disquietude as they went. At the same moment Crefton became aware that he was not the only human witness of the scene; a bent and withered old woman, whom he recognized at once as Martha Pillamon, of sinister reputation, had limped down the cottage path to the water's edge, and was gazing fixedly at the gruesome whirligig of dying birds that went in horrible procession round the pool. Presently her voice rang out in a shrill note of quavering rage:

' 'Tis Betsy Croot adone it, the old rat. I'll put a spell on her, see if I don't.'

Crefton slipped quietly away, uncertain whether or no the old woman had noticed his presence. Even before she had proclaimed the guiltiness of Betsy Croot, the latter's muttered incantation 'Let un sink as swims' had flashed uncomfortably across his mind. But it was the final threat of a retaliatory spell which crowded his mind with misgiving to the exclusion of all other thoughts or fancies. His reasoning powers could no longer afford to dismiss these old-wives' threats as empty bickerings. The household at Mowsle Barton lay under the displeasure of a vindictive old woman who seemed able to materialize her personal spites in a very practical fashion, and there was no saying what form her revenge for three drowned ducks might not take. As a member of the household Crefton might find himself involved in some general and highly disagreeable visitation of Martha Pillamon's wrath. Of course he knew that he was giving way to absurd fancies, but the behaviour of the spirit-lamp kettle and the subsequent scene at the pond had considerably unnerved him. And the vagueness of his alarm added to its terrors; when once you have taken the Impossible into your calculations its possibilities become practically limitless.

Crefton rose at his usual early hour the next morning, after one of the least restful nights he had spent at the farm. His sharpened senses quickly detected that subtle atmosphere of things-being-not-altogether well that hangs over a stricken household. The cows had been milked, but they stood huddled about in the yard, waiting impatiently to be driven out afield, and the poultry kept up an importunate querulous reminder of deferred feeding-time; the yard pump, which usually made discordant music at frequent intervals during the early morning, was today ominously silent. In the house itself there was a coming and going of scuttering footsteps, a rushing and dying away of hurried voices, and long, uneasy stillnesses. Crefton finished his dressing and made his way to the head of a narrow staircase. He could hear a dull, complaining voice, a voice into which an awed hush had crept, and recognized the speaker as Mrs Spurfield.

'He'll go away, for sure,' the voice was saying; 'there are those as runs away from one as soon as real misfortune shows itself.'

Crefton felt that he probably was one of 'those', and that there were moments when it was advisable to be true to type.

He crept back to his room, collected and packed his few belongings, placed the money due for his lodgings on a table, and made his way out by a back door into the yard. A mob of poultry surged expectantly towards him; shaking off their interested attentions he hurried along under cover of cowstall, piggery, and hayricks till he reached the lane at the back of the farm. A few minutes' walk, which only the burden of his portmanteaux restrained from developing into an undisguised run, brought him to a main road, where the early carrier soon overtook him and sped him onward to the neighbouring town. At a bend of the road he caught a last glimpse of the farm; the old gabled roofs and thatched barns, the straggling orchard, and the medlar tree, with its wooden seat, stood out with an almost spectral clearness in the early morning light, and over it all brooded that air of magic possession which Crefton had once mistaken for peace.

The bustle and roar of Paddington Station smote on his ears with a welcome protective greeting.

'Very bad for our nerves, all this rush and hurry,' said a fellow-traveller; 'give me the peace and quiet of the country.'

Crefton mentally surrendered his share of the desired commodity. A crowded, brilliantly over-lighted music-hall, where an exuberant rendering of '1812' was being given by a strenuous orchestra, came nearest to his ideal of a nerve sedative.

The Talking-Out of Tarrington

'Heavens!' exclaimed the aunt of Clovis, 'here's some one I know bearing down on us. I can't remember his name, but he lunched with us once in Town. Tarrington – yes, that's it. He's heard of the picnic I'm giving for the Princess, and he'll cling to me like a lifebelt till I give him an invitation; then he'll ask if he may bring all his wives and mothers and sisters with him. That's the worst of these small watering-places; one can't escape from anybody.'

'I'll fight a rearguard action for you if you like to do a bolt now,' volunteered Clovis; 'you've a clear ten yards start if you don't lose time.'

The aunt of Clovis responded gamely to the suggestion, and churned away like a Nile steamer, with a long brown ripple of Pekingese spaniel trailing in her wake.

'Pretend you don't know him,' was her parting advice, tinged with the reckless courage of the non-combatant.

The next moment the overtures of an affably disposed gentleman were being received by Clovis with a 'silent-upon-a-peak-in-Darien' stare which denoted an absence of all previous acquaintance with the object scrutinized.

'I expect you don't know me with my moustache,' said the newcomer; 'I've only grown it during the last two months.'

'On the contrary,' said Clovis, 'the moustache is the only thing about you that seemed familiar to me. I felt certain that I had met it somewhere before.'

'My name is Tarrington,' resumed the candidate for recognition.

'A very useful kind of name,' said Clovis; 'with a name of that sort no one would blame you if you did nothing in particular heroic or remarkable, would they? And yet if you were to raise a troop of light horse in a moment of national emergency, "Tarrington's Light Horse" would sound quite appropriate and pulse-quickening; whereas if you were called Spoopin, for instance, the thing would be out of the question. No one, even in a moment of national emergency, could possibly belong to Spoopin's Horse.'

The newcomer smiled weakly, as one who is not to be put off by mere flippancy, and began again with patient persistence:

'I think you ought to remember my name –'

'I shall,' said Clovis, with an air of immense sincerity. 'My aunt was asking me only this morning to suggest names for four young owls she's just had sent her as pets. I shall call them all Tarrington; then if one or two of them die or fly away, or leave us in any of the ways that pet owls are prone to, there will be always one or two left to carry on your name. And my aunt won't *let* me forget it; she will always be asking "Have the Tarringtons had their mice?" and questions of that sort. She says if you keep wild creatures in captivity you ought to see after their wants, and of course she's quite right there.'

'I met you at luncheon at your aunt's house once –' broke in Mr Tarrington, pale but still resolute.

'My aunt never lunches,' said Clovis; 'she belongs to the National Anti-Luncheon League, which is doing quite a lot of good work in a quiet, unobtrusive way. A subscription of half a crown per quarter entitles you to go without ninety-two luncheons.'

'This must be something new,' exclaimed Tarrington.

'It's the same aunt that I've always had,' said Clovis coldly.

'I perfectly well remember meeting you at a luncheon-party given by your aunt,' persisted Tarrington, who was beginning to flush an unhealthy shade of mottled pink.

'What was there for lunch?' asked Clovis.

'Oh, well, I don't remember that –'

'How nice of you to remember my aunt when you can no longer recall the names of the things you ate. Now my memory works quite differently. I can remember a menu long after I've forgotten the hostess that accompanied it. When I was seven years old I recollect being given a peach at a garden-party by some Duchess or other; I can't remember a thing about her, except that I imagine our acquaintance must have been of the slightest, as she called me a "nice little boy", but I have unfading memories of that peach. It was one of those exuberant peaches that meet you halfway, so to speak, and are all over you in a moment. It was a beautiful unspoiled product of a hot-house, and yet it managed quite successfully to give itself the airs of a compote. You had to bite it and imbibe it at the same time. To me there has always been something charming and mystic in the thought of that delicate velvet globe of fruit, slowly ripening and warming to perfection through the long summer days and perfumed nights, and then coming suddenly athwart my life in the supreme moment of its existence. I can never forget it, even if I wished to. And when I had devoured all that was edible of it, there still remained the stone, which a heedless, thoughtless child would doubtless have thrown away; I put it down the neck of a young friend who was wearing a very *décolleté* sailor suit. I told him it was a scorpion, and from the way he wriggled and screamed he evidently believed it, though where the silly kid imagined I could procure a live scorpion at a garden-party I don't know. Altogether, that peach is for me an unfading and happy memory –'

The defeated Tarrington had by this time retreated out of earshot, comforting himself as best he might with the reflection that a picnic which included the presence of Clovis might prove a doubtfully agreeable experience.

'I shall certainly go in for a Parliamentary career,' said Clovis to himself as he turned complacently to rejoin his aunt. 'As a talker-out of inconvenient bills I should be invaluable.'

The Hounds of Fate

In the fading light of a close dull autumn afternoon Martin Stoner plodded his way along muddy lanes and rut-seamed cart tracks that led he knew not exactly whither. Somewhere in front of him, he fancied, lay the sea, and towards the sea his footsteps seemed persistently turning; why he was struggling wearily forward to that goal he could scarcely have explained, unless he was possessed by the same instinct that turns a hard-pressed stag cliffward in its last extremity. In his case the hounds of Fate were certainly pressing him with unrelenting insistence; hunger, fatigue, and despairing hopelessness had numbed his brain, and he could scarcely summon sufficient energy to wonder what underlying impulse was driving him onward. Stoner was one of those unfortunate individuals who seem to have tried everything; a natural slothfulness and improvidence had always intervened to blight any chance of even moderate success, and now he was at the end of his tether, and there was nothing more to try. Desperation had not awakened in him any dormant reserve of energy; on the contrary, a mental torpor grew up round the crisis of his fortunes. With the clothes he stood up in, a halfpenny in his pocket, and no single friend or acquaintance to turn to, with no prospect either of a bed for the night or a meal for the morrow, Martin Stoner trudged stolidly forward, between moist hedge-rows and beneath dripping trees, his mind almost a blank, except that he was subconsciously aware that somewhere in front of him lay the sea. Another consciousness obtruded itself now and then – the knowledge that he was miserably hungry. Presently he came to a halt by an open gateway that led into a spacious and rather neg-lected farm-garden; there was little sign of life about, and the farm-house at the further end of the garden looked chill and inhospitable. A drizzling rain, however, was setting in, and Stoner thought that here perhaps he might obtain a few minutes' shelter and buy a glass of milk with his last remaining coin. He turned slowly and wearily into the garden and followed a narrow, flagged path up to a side door. Before he had time to knock the door opened and a bent, withered-looking old man stood aside in the doorway as though to let him pass in.

'Could I come in out of the rain?' Stoner began, but the old man interrupted him.

'Come in, Master Tom. I knew you would come back one of these days.'

Stoner lurched across the threshold and stood staring uncomprehendingly at the other.

'Sit down while I put you out a bit of supper,' said the old man with quavering eagerness. Stoner's legs gave way from very weariness, and he sank inertly into the armchair that had been pushed up to him. In another minute he was devouring the cold meat, cheese, and bread, that had been placed on the table at his side.

'You'm little changed these four years,' went on the old man, in a voice that sounded to Stoner as something in a dream, far away and inconsequent; 'but you'll find us a deal changed, you will. There's no one about the place same as when you left; nought but me and your old Aunt. I'll go and tell her that you'm come; she won't be seeing you, but she'll let you stay right enough. She always did say if you was to come back you should stay, but she'd never set eyes on you or speak to you again.'

The old man placed a mug of beer on the table in front of Stoner and then hobbled away down a long passage. The drizzle of rain had changed to a furious lashing downpour, which beat violently against door and windows. The wanderer thought with a shudder of what the sea-shore must look like under this drenching rainfall, with night beating down on all sides. He finished the food and beer and sat numbly waiting for the return of his strange host. As the minutes ticked by on the grandfather clock in the corner a new hope began to flicker and grow in the young man's mind; it was merely the expansion of his former craving for food and a few minutes' rest into a longing to find a night's shelter under this seemingly hospitable roof. A clattering of footsteps down the passage heralded the old farm servant's return.

'The old Missus won't see you, Master Tom, but she says you are to stay. 'Tis right enough, seeing the farm will be yours when she be put under earth. I've had a fire lit in your room, Master Tom, and the maids has put fresh sheets on to the bed. You'll find nought changed up there. Maybe you'm tired and would like to go there now.'

Without a word Martin Stoner rose heavily to his feet and followed his ministering angel along a passage, up a short creaking stair, along another passage, and into a large room lit with a cheerfully blazing fire. There was but little furniture, plain, old-fashioned, and good of its kind; a stuffed squirrel in a case and a wall-calendar of four years ago were about the only symptoms of decoration. But Stoner had eyes for little else than the bed, and could scarce wait to tear his clothes off him before rolling in a luxury of weariness into its comfortable depths. The hounds of Fate seemed to have checked for a brief moment.

In the cold light of morning Stoner laughed mirthlessly as he slowly realized the position in which he found himself. Perhaps he might snatch a bit of breakfast on the strength of his likeness to this other missing ne'er-do-well, and get safely away before anyone discovered the fraud that had been thrust on him. In the room downstairs he found the bent old man ready with a dish of bacon and fried eggs for 'Master Tom's' breakfast, while a hard-faced elderly maid brought in a teapot and poured him out a cup of tea. As he sat at the table a small spaniel came up and made friendly advances.

' 'Tis old Bowker's pup,' explained the old man, whom the hard-faced maid had addressed as George. 'She was main fond of you; never seemed the same after you went away to Australee. She died 'bout a year agone. 'Tis her pup.'

Stoner found it difficult to regret her decease; as a witness for identification she would have left something to be desired.

'You'll go for a ride, Master Tom?' was the next start-ling proposition that came from the old man. 'We've a nice little roan cob that goes well in saddle. Old Biddy is getting a bit up in years, though 'er goes well still, but I'll have the little roan saddled and brought round to door.'

'I've got no riding things,' stammered the castaway, almost laughing as he looked down at his one suit of well-worn clothes.

'Master Tom,' said the old man earnestly, almost with an offended air, 'all your things is just as you left them. A bit of airing before the fire an' they'll be all right. 'Twill be a bit of a distraction like, a little riding and wild-fowling now and agen. You'll find the folk around here has hard and bitter minds towards you. They hasn't for-gotten nor forgiven. No one'll come nigh you, so you'd best get what distraction you can with horse and dog. They'm good company, too.'

Old George hobbled away to give his orders, and Stoner, feeling more than ever like one in a dream, went upstairs to inspect 'Master Tom's' wardrobe. A ride was one of the pleasures dearest to his heart, and there was some protection against immediate discovery of his imposture in the thought that none of Tom's aforetime companions were likely to favour him with a close inspection. As the interloper thrust himself into some tolerably well-fitting riding cords he wondered vaguely what manner of misdeed the genuine Tom had committed to set the whole countryside against him. The thud of quick, eager hoofs on damp earth cut short his speculations. The roan cob had been brought up to the side door.

'Talk of beggars on horseback,' thought Stoner to himself, as he trotted rapidly along the muddy lanes where he had tramped yesterday as a down-at-heel outcast; and then he flung reflection indolently aside and gave himself up to the pleasure of a smart canter along the turf-grown side of a level stretch of road. At an open gateway he checked his pace to allow two carts to turn into a field. The lads driving the carts found time to give him a prolonged stare, and as he passed on he heard an excited voice call out, ' 'Tis Tom Prike! I knowed him at once; showing hisself here agen, is he?'

Evidently the likeness which had imposed at close

quarters on a doddering old man was good enough to mislead younger eyes at a short distance.

In the course of his ride he met with ample evidence to confirm the statement that local folk had neither forgotten nor forgiven the bygone crime which had come to him as a legacy from the absent Tom. Scowling looks, mutterings, and nudgings greeted him whenever he chanced upon human beings; 'Bowker's pup', trotting placidly by his side, seemed the one element of friendliness in a hostile world.

As he dismounted at the side door he caught a fleeting glimpse of a gaunt, elderly woman peering at him from behind the curtain of an upper window. Evidently this was his aunt by adoption.

Over the ample midday meal that stood in readiness for him Stoner was able to review the possibilities of his extraordinary situation. The real Tom, after four years of absence, might suddenly turn up at the farm, or a letter might come from him at any moment. Again, in the character of heir to the farm, the false Tom might be called on to sign documents, which would be an embarrassing predicament. Or a relative might arrive who would not imitate the aunt's attitude of aloofness. All these things would mean ignominious exposure. On the other hand, the alternatives were the open sky and the muddy lanes that led down to the sea. The farm offered him, at any rate, a temporary refuge from destitution; farming was one of the many things he had 'tried', and he would be able to do a certain amount of work in return for the hospitality to which he was so little entitled.

'Will you have cold pork for your supper,' asked the hard-faced maid, as she cleared the table, 'or will you have it hotted up?'

'Hot, with onions,' said Stoner. It was the only time in his life that he had made a rapid decision. And as he gave the order he knew that he meant to stay.

Stoner kept rigidly to those portions of the house which seemed to have been allotted to him by a tacit treaty of delimitation. When he took part in the farm-work it was as one who worked under orders and never initiated them. Old George, the roan cob, and Bowker's pup were his sole companions in a world that was other-wise frostily silent and hostile. Of the mistress of the farm he saw nothing. Once, when he knew she had gone forth to church, he made a furtive visit to the farm parlour in an endeavour to glean some fragmentary knowledge of the young man whose place he had usurped, and whose ill-repute he had fastened on himself. There were many photographs hung on the walls, or stuck in prim frames, but the likeness he sought for was not among them. At last, in an album thrust out of sight, he came across what he wanted. There was a whole series, labelled 'Tom', a podgy child of three, in a fantastic frock, an awkward boy of about twelve, holding a cricket bat as though he loathed it, a rather good-looking youth of eighteen with very smooth, evenly parted hair, and, finally, a young man with a somewhat surly dare-devil expression. At this last portrait Stoner looked with particular interest; the likeness to himself was unmistakable.

From the lips of old George, who was garrulous enough on most subjects, he tried again and again to learn something of the nature of the offence which shut him off as a creature to be shunned and hated by his fellow-men.

'What do the folk around here say about me?' he asked one day as they were walking home from an outlying field.

The old man shook his head.

'They be bitter agen you, mortal bitter. Ay, 'tis a sad business, a sad business.'

And never could he be got to say anything more enlightening.

On a clear frosty evening, a few days before the festival of Christmas, Stoner stood in a corner of the orchard which commanded a wide view of the countryside. Here and there he could see the twinkling dots of lamp or candle glow which told of human homes where the goodwill and jollity of the season held their sway. Behind him lay the grim, silent farm-house, where no one ever laughed, where even a quarrel would have seemed cheerful. As he turned to look at the long grey front of the gloom-shadowed building, a door opened and old George came hurriedly forth. Stoner heard his adopted name called in a tone of strained anxiety. Instantly he knew that something untoward had happened, and with a quick revulsion of outlook his sanctuary became in his eyes a place of peace and contentment, from which he dreaded to be driven.

'Master Tom,' said the old man in a hoarse whisper, 'you must slip away quiet from here for a few days. Michael Ley is back in the village, an' he swears to shoot you if he can come across you. He'll do it, too, there's murder in the look of him. Get away under cover of night, 'tis only for a week or so, he won't be here longer.'

'But where am I to go?' stammered Stoner, who had caught the infection of the old man's obvious terror.

'Go right away along the coast to Punchford and keep hid there. When Michael's safe gone I'll ride the roan over to the Green Dragon at Punchford; when you see the cob stabled at the Green Dragon 'tis a sign you may come back agen.'

'But –' began Stoner hesitatingly.

' 'Tis all right for money,' said the other; 'the old Missus agrees you'd best do as I say, and she's given me this.'

The old man produced three sovereigns and some odd silver.

Stoner felt more of a cheat than ever as he stole away that night from the back gate of the farm with the old woman's money in his pocket. Old George and Bowker's pup stood watching him a silent farewell from the yard. He could scarcely fancy that he would ever come back, and he felt a throb of compunction for those two humble friends who would wait wistfully for his return. Some day perhaps the real Tom would come back, and there would be wild wonderment among those simple farm folks as to the identity of the shadowy guest they had harboured under their roof. For his own fate he felt no immediate anxiety; three pounds goes but little way in the world when there is nothing behind it, but to a man who has counted his exchequer in pennies it seems a good starting-point. Fortune had done him a whimsically kind turn when last he trod these lanes as a hopeless adventurer, and there might yet be a chance of his finding some work and making a fresh start; as he got further from the farm his spirits rose higher. There was a sense of relief in regaining once more his lost identity and ceasing to be the uneasy ghost of another. He scarcely bothered to speculate about the implacable enemy who had dropped from nowhere into his life; since that life was now behind him one unreal item the more made little difference. For the first time for many months he began to hum a careless light-hearted refrain. Then there stepped out from the shadow of an overhanging oak tree a man with a gun. There was no need to wonder who he might be; the moonlight falling on his white set face revealed a glare of human hate such as Stoner in the ups and downs of his wanderings had never seen before. He sprang aside in a wild effort to break through the hedge that bordered the lane, but the tough branches held him fast. The hounds of Fate had waited for him in those narrow lanes, and this time they were not to be denied.

The Remoulding of Groby Lington

'A man is known by the company he keeps.'

In the morning-room of his sister-in-law's house Groby Lington fidgeted away the passing minutes with the demure restlessness of advanced middle age. About a quarter of an hour would have to elapse before it would be time to say his good-byes and make his way across the village green to the station, with a selected escort of nephews and nieces. He was a good-natured, kindly dispositioned man, and in theory he was delighted to pay periodical visits to the wife and children of his dead brother William; in practice, he infinitely preferred the comfort and seclusion of his own house and garden, and the companionship of his books and his parrot to these rather meaningless and tiresome incursions into a family circle with which he had little in common. It was not so much the spur of his own conscience that drove him to make the occasional short journey by rail to visit his relatives, as an obedient concession to the more insistent but

167

vicarious conscience of his brother, Colonel John, who was apt to accuse him of neglecting poor old William's family. Groby usually forgot or ignored the existence of his neighbour kinsfolk until such time as he was threatened with a visit from the Colonel, when he would put matters straight by a hurried pilgrimage across the few miles of intervening country to renew his acquaintance with the young people and assume a kindly if rather forced interest in the well-being of his sister-in-law. On this occasion he had cut matters so fine between the timing of his exculpatory visit and the coming of Colonel John, that he would scarcely be home before the latter was due to arrive. Anyhow, Groby had got it over, and six or seven months might decently elapse before he need again sacrifice his comforts and inclinations on the altar of family sociability. He was inclined to be distinctly cheerful as he hopped about the room, picking up first one object, then another, and subjecting each to a brief bird-like scrutiny.

Presently his cheerful listlessness changed sharply to an attitude of vexed attention. In a scrap-book of drawings and caricatures belonging to one of his nephews he had come across an unkindly clever sketch of himself and his parrot, solemnly confronting each other in postures of ridiculous gravity and repose, and bearing a likeness to one another that the artist had done his utmost to accentuate. After the first flush of annoyance had passed away, Groby laughed good-naturedly and admitted to himself the cleverness of the drawing. Then the feeling of resentment repossessed him, resentment not against the caricaturist who had embodied the idea in pen and ink, but against the possible truth that the idea represented. Was it really the case that people grew in time to resemble the animals they kept as pets, and had he unconsciously become more and more like the comically solemn bird that was his constant companion? Groby was unusually silent as he walked to the train with his escort of chattering nephews and nieces, and during the short railway journey his mind was more and more possessed with an introspective conviction that he had gradually settled down into a sort of parrot-like existence. What, after all, did his daily routine amount to but a sedate meandering and pecking and perching, in his garden, among his fruit trees, in his wicker chair on the lawn, or by the fireside in his library? And what was the sum total of his conversation with chance-encountered neighbours? 'Quite a spring day, isn't it?' 'It looks as though we should have some rain.' 'Glad to see you about again; you must take care of yourself.' 'How the young folk shoot up, don't they?' Strings of stupid, inevitable perfunctory remarks came to his mind, remarks that were certainly not the mental exchange of human intelligences, but mere empty parrot-talk. One might really just as well salute one's acquaintances with 'Pretty Polly. Puss, puss, miaow!' Groby began to fume against the picture of himself as a foolish feathered fowl which his nephew's sketch had first suggested, and which his own accusing imagination was filling in with such unflattering detail.

'I'll give the beastly bird away,' he said resentfully; though he knew at the same time that he would do no such thing. It would look so absurd after all the years that he had kept the parrot and made much of it suddenly to try and find it a new home.

'Has my brother arrived?' he asked of the stable-boy, who had come with the pony-carriage to meet him.

'Yessir, came down by the two-fifteen. Your parrot's dead.' The boy made the latter announcement with the relish which his class finds in proclaiming a catastrophe.

'My parrot dead?' said Groby. 'What caused its death?'

'The ipe,' said the boy briefly.

'The ipe?' queried Groby. 'Whatever's that?'

'The ipe what the Colonel brought down with him,' came the rather alarming answer.

'Do you mean to say my brother is ill?' asked Groby. 'Is it something infectious?'

'Th' Colonel's so well as ever he was,' said the boy; and as no further explanation was forthcoming Groby had to possess himself in mystified patience till he reached home. His brother was waiting for him at the hall door.

'Have you heard about the parrot?' he asked at once. ' 'Pon my soul I'm awfully sorry. The moment he saw the monkey I'd brought down as a surprise for you he squawked out, "Rats to you, sir!", and the blessed monkey made one spring at him, got him by the neck and whirled him round like a rattle. He was as dead as mutton by the time I'd got him out of the little beggar's paws. Always been such a friendly little beast, the monkey has, should never have thought he'd got it in him to see red like that. Can't tell you how sorry I feel about it, and now of course you'll hate the sight of the monkey.'

'Not at all,' said Groby sincerely. A few hours earlier the tragic end which had befallen his parrot would have presented itself to him as a calamity; now it arrived almost as a polite attention on the part of the Fates.

'The bird was getting old, you know,' he went on, in explanation of his obvious lack of decent regret at the loss of his pet. 'I was really beginning to wonder if it was an unmixed kindness to let him go on living till he succumbed to old age. What a charming little monkey!' he added, when he was introduced to the culprit.

The newcomer was a small, long-tailed monkey from the Western Hemisphere, with a gentle, half-shy, half-trusting manner that instantly captured Groby's confidence; a student of simian character might have seen in the fitful red light in its eyes some indication of the underlying temper which the parrot had so rashly put to the test with such dramatic consequences for itself. The servants, who had come to regard the defunct bird as a regular member of the household, and one who gave really very little trouble, were scandalized to find his bloodthirsty aggressor installed in his place as an honoured domestic pet.

'A nasty heathen ipe what don't never say nothing sensible and cheerful, same as pore Polly did,' was the unfavourable verdict of the kitchen quarters.

One Sunday morning, some twelve or fourteen months after the visit of Colonel John and the parrot-tragedy, Miss Wepley sat decorously in her pew in the parish church, immediately in front of that occupied by Groby Lington. She was, comparatively speaking, a newcomer in the neighbourhood, and was not personally acquainted with her fellow-worshipper in the seat behind, but for the past two years the Sunday morning service had brought them regularly within each other's sphere of consciousness. Without having paid particular attention to the subject, she could probably have given a correct rendering of the way in which he pronounced certain words occurring in the responses, while he was well aware of the trivial fact that, in addition to her prayer book and handkerchief, a small paper packet of throat lozenges always reposed on the seat beside her. Miss Wepley rarely had recourse to her lozenges, but in case she should be taken with a fit of coughing she wished to have the emergency duly provided for. On this particular Sunday the lozenges occasioned an unusual diversion in the even tenor of her devotions, far more disturbing to her personally than a prolonged attack of coughing would have been. As she rose to take part in the singing of the first hymn, she fancied that she saw the hand of her neighbour, who was alone in the pew behind her, make a furtive downward grab at the packet lying on the seat; on turning sharply round she found that the packet had certainly disappeared, but Mr Lington was to all outward seeming serenely intent on his hymn-book. No amount of interrogatory glaring on the part of the despoiled lady could bring the least shade of conscious guilt to his face.

'Worse was to follow,' as she remarked afterwards to a scandalized audience of friends and acquaintances. 'I had scarcely knelt in prayer when a lozenge, one of *my* lozenges, came whizzing into the pew, just under my nose. I turned round and stared, but Mr Lington had his eyes closed and his lips moving as though engaged in prayer. The moment I resumed my devotions another lozenge came rattling in, and then another. I took no notice for a while, and then turned round suddenly just as the dreadful man was about to flip another one at me. He hastily pretended to be turning over the leaves of his book, but I was not to be taken in that time. He saw that he had been discovered and no more lozenges came. Of course I have changed my pew.'

'No gentleman would have acted in such a disgraceful manner,' said one of her listeners; 'and yet Mr Lington used to be so respected by everybody. He seems to have behaved like a little ill-bred schoolboy.'

'He behaved like a monkey,' said Miss Wepley.

Her unfavourable verdict was echoed in other quarters about the same time. Groby Lington had never been a hero in the eyes of his personal retainers, but he had shared the approval accorded to his defunct parrot as a cheerful, well-dispositioned body, who gave no particular trouble. Of late months, however, this character would hardly have been endorsed by the members of his domestic establishment. The stolid stable-boy, who had first announced to him the tragic end of his feathered pet, was one of the first to give voice to the murmurs of disapproval which became rampant and general in the servants' quarters, and he had fairly substantial grounds for his disaffection. In a burst of hot summer weather he had obtained permission to bathe in a modest-sized pond in the orchard, and thither one afternoon Groby had bent his steps, attracted by loud imprecations of anger mingled with the shriller chattering of monkey-language. He beheld his plump diminutive servitor, clad only in a waistcoat and a pair of socks, storming ineffectually at the monkey which was seated on a low branch of an apple tree, abstractedly fingering the remainder of the boy's outfit, which he had removed just out of his reach.

'The ipe's been an' took my clothes,' whined the boy, with the passion of his kind for explaining the obvious. His incomplete toilet effect rather embarrassed him, but he hailed the arrival of Groby with relief, as promising moral and material support in his efforts to get back his raided garments. The monkey had ceased its defiant jabbering, and doubtless with a little coaxing from its master it would hand back the plunder.

'If I lift you up,' suggested Groby, 'you will just be able to reach the clothes.'

The boy agreed, and Groby clutched him firmly by the waistcoat, which was about all there was to catch hold of, and lifted him clear of the ground. Then, with a deft swing he sent him crashing into a clump of tall nettles, which closed receptively round him. The victim had not been brought up in a school which teaches one to repress one's emotions – if a fox had attempted to gnaw at his vitals he would have flown to complain to the nearest hunt committee rather than have affected an attitude of stoical indifference. On this occasion the volume of sound which he produced under the stimulus of pain and rage and astonishment was generous and sustained, but above his bellowings he could distinctly hear the triumphant chattering of his enemy in the tree, and a peal of shrill laughter from Groby.

When the boy had finished an improvised St Vitus caracole, which would have brought him fame on the boards of the Coliseum, and which indeed met with ready appreciation and applause from the retreating figure of Groby Lington, he found that the monkey had also discreetly retired, while his clothes were scattered on the grass at the foot of the tree.

'They'm two ipes, that's what they be,' he muttered angrily, and if his judgment was severe, at least he spoke under the sting of considerable provocation.

It was a week or two later that the parlour-maid gave

notice, having been terrified almost to tears by an outbreak of sudden temper on the part of the master anent
some under done cutlets. ' 'E gnashed 'is teeth at me,
'e did reely,' she informed a sympathetic kitchen
audience.

'I'd like to see 'im talk like that to me, I would,' said
the cook defiantly, but her cooking from that moment
showed a marked improvement.

It was seldom that Groby Lington so far detached
himself from his accustomed habits as to go and form one
of a house-party, and he was not a little piqued that Mrs
Glenduff should have stowed him away in the musty old
Georgian wing of the house, in the next room, moreover,
to Leonard Spabbink, the eminent pianist.

'He plays Liszt like an angel,' had been the hostess's
enthusiastic testimonial.

'He may play him like a trout for all I care,' had been
Groby's mental comment, 'but I wouldn't mind betting
that he snores. He's just the sort and shape that would.
And if I hear him snoring through those ridiculous thin-
panelled walls, there'll be trouble.'

He did, and there was.

Groby stood it for about two and a quarter minutes,
and then made his way through the corridor into Spabbink's room. Under Groby's vigorous measures the
musician's flabby, redundant figure sat up in bewildered
semi-consciousness like an ice-cream that has been taught
to beg. Groby prodded him into complete wakefulness,

and then the pettish self-satisfied pianist fairly lost his temper and slapped his domineering visitant on the hand. In another moment Spabbink was being nearly stifled and very effectually gagged by a pillow-case tightly bound round his head, while his plump pyjama'd limbs were hauled out of bed and smacked, pinched, kicked, and bumped in a catch-as-catch-can progress across the floor, towards the flat shallow bath in whose utterly inadequate depths Groby perseveringly strove to drown him. For a few moments the room was almost in darkness: Groby's candle had overturned in an early stage of the scuffle, and its flicker scarcely reached to the spot where splashings, smacks, muffled cries, and splutterings, and a chatter of ape-like rage told of the struggle that was being waged round the shores of the bath. A few instants later the one-sided combat was brightly lit up by the flare of blazing curtains and rapidly kindling panelling.

When the hastily aroused members of the house-party stampeded out on to the lawn, the Georgian wing was well alight and belching forth masses of smoke, but some moments elapsed before Groby appeared with the half-drowned pianist in his arms, having just bethought him of the superior drowning facilities offered by the pond at the bottom of the lawn. The cool night air sobered his rage, and when he found that he was innocently acclaimed as the heroic rescuer of poor Leonard Spabbink, and loudly commended for his presence of mind in tying a wet cloth round his head to protect him from smoke suffocation, he accepted the situation, and subsequently gave a graphic account of his finding the musician asleep with an overturned candle by his side and the conflagration well started. Spabbink gave *his* version some days later, when he had partially recovered from the shock of his midnight castigation and immersion, but the gentle pitying smiles and evasive comments with which his story was greeted warned him that the public ear was not at his disposal. He refused, however, to attend the ceremonial presentation of the Royal Humane Society's life-saving medal.

It was about this time that Groby's pet monkey fell a victim to the disease which attacks so many of its kind when brought under the influence of a northern climate. Its master appeared to be profoundly affected by its loss, and never quite recovered the level of spirits that he had recently attained. In company with the tortoise, which Colonel John presented to him on his last visit, he potters about his lawn and kitchen garden, with none of his erstwhile sprightliness; and his nephews and nieces are fairly well justified in alluding to him as 'Old Uncle Groby'.

The Open Window

'My aunt will be down presently, Mr Nuttel,' said a very self-possessed young lady of fifteen; 'in the meantime you must try and put up with me.'

Framton Nuttel endeavoured to say the correct something which should duly flatter the niece of the moment without unduly discounting the aunt that was to come. Privately he doubted more than ever whether these formal visits on a succession of total strangers would do much towards helping the nerve cure which he was supposed to be undergoing.

'I know how it will be,' his sister had said when he was preparing to migrate to this rural retreat; 'you will bury yourself down there and not speak to a living soul, and your nerves will be worse than ever from moping. I shall just give you letters of introduction to all the people I know there. Some of them, as far as I can remember, were quite nice.'

Framton wondered whether Mrs Sappleton, the lady

to whom he was presenting one of the letters of introduction, came into the nice division.

'Do you know many of the people round here?' asked the niece, when she judged that they had had sufficient silent communion.

'Hardly a soul,' said Framton. 'My sister was staying here, at the rectory, you know, some four years ago, and she gave me letters of introduction to some of the people here.'

He made the last statement in a tone of distinct regret.

'Then you know practically nothing about my aunt?' pursued the self-possessed young lady.

'Only her name and address,' admitted the caller. He was wondering whether Mrs Sappleton was in the married or widowed state. An undefinable something about the room seemed to suggest masculine habitation.

'Her great tragedy happened just three years ago,' said the child; 'that would be since your sister's time.'

'Her tragedy?' asked Framton; somehow in this restful country spot tragedies seemed out of place.

'You may wonder why we keep that window wide open on an October afternoon,' said the niece, indicating a large French window that opened on to a lawn.

'It is quite warm for the time of the year,' said Framton; 'but has that window got anything to do with the tragedy?'

'Out through that window, three years ago to a day, her husband and her two young brothers went off for their day's shooting. They never came back. In crossing the moor to their favourite snipe-shooting ground they were all three engulfed in a treacherous piece of bog. It had been that dreadful wet summer, you know, and places that were safe in other years gave way suddenly without warning. Their bodies were never recovered. That was the dreadful part of it.' Here the child's voice lost its self-possessed note and became falteringly human. 'Poor aunt always thinks that they will come back some day, they and the little brown spaniel that was lost with them, and walk in at that window just as they used to do. That is why the window is kept open every evening till it is quite dusk. Poor dear aunt, she has often told me how they went out, her husband with his white waterproof coat over his arm, and Ronnie, her youngest brother, singing, "Bertie, why do you bound?" as he always did to tease her, because she said it got on her nerves. Do you know, sometimes on still, quiet evenings like this, I almost get a creepy feeling that they will all walk in through that window –'

She broke off with a little shudder. It was a relief to Framton when the aunt bustled into the room with a whirl of apologies for being late in making her appearance.

'I hope Vera has been amusing you?' she said.

'She has been very interesting,' said Framton.

'I hope you don't mind the open window,' said Mrs Sappleton briskly; 'my husband and brothers will be home directly from shooting, and they always come in this way. They've been out for snipe in the marshes today, so they'll make a fine mess over my poor carpets. So like you men-folk, isn't it?'

She rattled on cheerfully about the shooting and the scarcity of birds, and the prospects for duck in the winter. To Framton, it was all purely horrible. He made a desperate but only partially successful effort to turn the talk on to a less ghastly topic; he was conscious that his hostess was giving him only a fragment of her attention, and her eyes were constantly straying past him to the open window and the lawn beyond. It was certainly an unfortunate coincidence that he should have paid his visit on this tragic anniversary.

'The doctors agree in ordering me complete rest, an absence of mental excitement, and avoidance of anything in the nature of violent physical exercise,' announced Framton, who laboured under the tolerably wide-spread delusion that total strangers and chance acquaintances are hungry for the least detail of one's ailments and infirmities, their cause and cure. 'On the matter of diet they are not so much in agreement,' he continued.

'No?' said Mrs Sappleton, in a voice which only replaced a yawn at the last moment. Then she suddenly brightened into alert attention – but not to what Framton was saying.

'Here they are at last!' she cried. 'Just in time for tea, and don't they look as if they were muddy up to the eyes!'

Framton shivered slightly and turned towards the niece with a look intended to convey sympathetic comprehension. The child was staring out through the open window with dazed horror in her eyes. In a chill shock of nameless fear Framton swung round in his seat and looked in the same direction.

In the deepening twilight three figures were walking across the lawn towards the window; they all carried guns under their arms, and one of them was additionally burdened with a white coat hung over his shoulders. A tired brown spaniel kept close at their heels. Noiselessly they neared the house, and then a hoarse young voice chanted out of the dusk: 'I said, Bertie, why do you bound?'

Framton grabbed wildly at his stick and hat; the hall-door, the gravel-drive, and the front gate were dimly noted stages in his headlong retreat. A cyclist coming along the road had to run into the hedge to avoid imminent collision.

'Here we are, my dear,' said the bearer of the white mackintosh, coming in through the window; 'fairly muddy, but most of it's dry. Who was that who bolted out as we came up?'

'A most extraordinary man, a Mr Nuttel,' said Mrs Sappleton; 'could only talk about his illnesses, and dashed off without a word of good-bye or apology when you arrived. One would think he had seen a ghost.'

'I expect it was the spaniel,' said the niece calmly; 'he told me he had a horror of dogs. He was once hunted into a cemetery somewhere on the banks of the Ganges by a pack of pariah dogs, and had to spend the night in a newly dug grave with the creatures snarling and grinning and foaming just above him. Enough to make any one lose their nerve.'

Romance at short notice was her speciality.

The Schartz-Metterklume Method

Lady Carlotta stepped out on to the platform of the small wayside station and took a turn or two up and down its uninteresting length, to kill time till the train should be pleased to proceed on its way. Then, in the roadway beyond, she saw a horse struggling with a more than ample load, and a carter of the sort that seems to bear a sullen hatred against the animal that helps him to earn a living. Lady Carlotta promptly betook her to the roadway, and put rather a different complexion on the struggle. Certain of her acquaintances were wont to give her plentiful admonition as to the undesirability of interfering on behalf of a distressed animal, such interference being 'none of her business.' Only once had she put the doctrine of non-interference into practice, when one of its most eloquent exponents had been besieged for nearly three hours in a small and extremely uncomfortable may-tree by an angry boar-pig, while Lady Carlotta, on the other side of the fence, had proceeded with the water-colour sketch she was engaged on, and refused to interfere between the boar and his prisoner. It is to be feared that she lost the friendship of the ultimately rescued lady. On this occasion she merely lost the train, which gave way to the first sign of impatience it had shown throughout the journey, and steamed off without her. She bore the desertion with philosophical indifference; her friends and relations were thoroughly well used to the fact of her luggage arriving without her. She wired a vague noncommittal message to her destination to say that she was coming on 'by another train.' Before she had time to think what her next move might be she was confronted by an imposingly attired lady, who seemed to be taking a prolonged mental inventory of her clothes and looks.

'You must be Miss Hope, the governess I've come to meet,' said the apparition, in a tone that admitted of very little argument.

'Very well, if I must I must,' said Lady Carlotta to herself with dangerous meekness.

'I am Mrs Quabarl,' continued the lady; 'and where, pray, is your luggage?'

'It's gone astray,' said the alleged governess, falling in with the excellent rule of life that the absent are always to blame; the luggage had, in point of fact, behaved with perfect correctitude. 'I've just telegraphed about it,' she added, with a nearer approach to truth.

'How provoking,' said Mrs Quabarl; 'these railway companies are so careless. However, my maid can lend you things for the night,' and she led the way to her car.

During the drive to the Quabarl mansion Lady Carlotta was impressively introduced to the nature of the charge that had been thrust upon her; she learned that Claude and Wilfrid were delicate, sensitive young people, that Irene had the artistic temperament highly developed, and that Viola was something or other else of a mould equally commonplace among children of that class and type in the twentieth century.

'I wish them not only to be *taught*,' said Mrs Quabarl, 'but *interested* in what they learn. In their history lessons, for instance, you must try to make them feel that they are being introduced to the life-stories of men and women who really lived, not merely committing a mass of names and dates to memory. French, of course, I shall expect you to talk at mealtimes several days in the week.'

'I shall talk French four days of the week and Russian in the remaining three.'

'Russian? My dear Miss Hope, no one in the house speaks or understands Russian.'

'That will not embarrass me in the least,' said Lady Carlotta coldly.

Mrs Quabarl, to use a colloquial expression, was knocked off her perch. She was one of those imperfectly self-assured individuals who are magnificent and autocratic as long as they are not seriously opposed. The least show of unexpected resistance goes a long way towards rendering them cowed and apologetic. When the new governess failed to express wondering admiration of the large newly purchased and expensive car, and lightly alluded to the superior advantages of one or two makes which had just been put on the market, the discomfiture of her patroness became almost abject. Her feelings were those which might have animated a general of ancient warfaring days, on beholding his heaviest battle-elephant ignominiously driven off the field by slingers and javelin throwers.

At dinner that evening, although reinforced by her husband, who usually duplicated her opinions and lent her moral support generally, Mrs Quabarl regained none of her lost ground. The governess not only helped herself well and truly to wine, but held forth with considerable show of critical knowledge on various vintage matters, concerning which the Quabarls were in no wise able to pose as authorities. Previous governesses had limited their conversation on the wine topic to a respectful and doubtless sincere expression of a preference for water. When this one went as far as to recommend a wine firm in whose hands you could not go very far wrong Mrs Quabarl thought it time to turn the conversation into more usual channels.

'We got very satisfactory references about you from Canon Teep,' she observed; 'a very estimable man, I should think.'

'Drinks like a fish and beats his wife, otherwise a very lovable character,' said the governess imperturbably.

'My *dear* Miss Hope! I trust you are exaggerating,' exclaimed the Quabarls in unison.

'One must in justice admit that there is some provocation,' continued the romancer. 'Mrs Teep is quite the most irritating bridge-player that I have ever sat down with; her leads and declarations would condone a certain amount of brutality in her partner, but to souse her with the contents of the only soda-water syphon in the house on a Sunday afternoon, when one couldn't get another, argues an indifference to the comfort of others which I cannot altogether overlook. You may think me hasty in my judgments, but it was practically on account of the syphon incident that I left.'

'We will talk of this some other time,' said Mrs Quabarl hastily.

'I shall never allude to it again,' said the governess with decision.

Mr Quabarl made a welcome diversion by asking what studies the new instructress proposed to inaugurate on the morrow.

'History to begin with,' she informed him.

'Ah, history,' he observed sagely; 'now in teaching them history you must take care to interest them in what they learn. You must make them feel that they are being introduced to the life-stories of men and women who really lived –'

'I've told her all that,' interposed Mrs Quabarl.

'I teach history on the Schartz-Metterklume method,' said the governess loftily.

'Ah, yes,' said her listeners, thinking it expedient to assume an acquaintance at least with the name.

'What are you children doing out here?' demanded Mrs Quabarl the next morning, on finding Irene sitting rather glumly at the head of the stairs, while her sister was perched in an attitude of depressed discomfort on the window-seat behind her, with a wolf-skin rug almost covering her.

'We are having a history lesson,' came the unexpected reply. 'I am supposed to be Rome, and Viola up there is the she-wolf; not a real wolf, but the figure of one that the Romans used to set store by – I forget why. Claude and Wilfrid have gone to fetch the shabby women.'

'The shabby women?'

'Yes, they've got to carry them off. They didn't want to, but Miss Hope got one of father's fives-bats and said she'd give them a number nine spanking if they didn't, so they've gone to do it.'

A loud, angry screaming from the direction of the lawn drew Mrs Quabarl thither in hot haste, fearful lest the threatened castigation might even now be in process of infliction. The outcry, however, came principally from the two small daughters of the lodge-keeper, who were being hauled and pushed towards the house by the panting and dishevelled Claude and Wilfrid, whose task was rendered even more arduous by the incessant, if not very effectual, attacks of the captured maidens' small brother. The governess, fives-bat in hand, sat negligently on the stone balustrade, presiding over the scene with the cold impartiality of a Goddess of Battles. A furious and repeated chorus of 'I'll tell muvver' rose from the lodge children, but the lodge-mother, who was hard of hearing, was for the moment-immersed in the preoccupation of her washtub. After an apprehensive glance in the direction of the lodge (the good woman was gifted with the highly militant temper which is sometimes the privilege of deafness) Mrs Quabarl flew indignantly to the rescue of the struggling captives.

'Wilfrid! Claude! Let those children go at once. Miss Hope, what on earth is the meaning of this scene?'

'Early Roman history; the Sabine women, don't you know? It's the Schartz-Metterklume method to make children understand history by acting it themselves; fixes it in their memory, you know. Of course, if, thanks to your interference, your boys go through life thinking that the Sabine women ultimately escaped, I really cannot be held responsible.'

'You may be very clever and modern, Miss Hope,' said Mrs Quabarl firmly, 'but I should like you to leave here by the next train. Your luggage will be sent after you as soon as it arrives.'

'I'm not certain exactly where I shall be for the next few days,' said the dismissed instructress of youth; 'you might keep my luggage till I wire my address. There are only a couple of trunks and some golf-clubs and a leopard cub.'

'A leopard cub!' gasped Mrs Quabarl. Even in her departure this extraordinary person seemed destined to leave a trail of embarrassment behind her.

'Well, it's rather left off being a cub; it's more than half-grown, you know. A fowl every day and a rabbit on Sundays is what it usually gets. Raw beef makes it too excitable. Don't trouble about getting the car for me, I'm rather inclined for a walk.'

And Lady Carlotta strode out of the Quabarl horizon.

The advent of the genuine Miss Hope, who had made a mistake as to the day on which she was due to arrive, caused a turmoil which that good lady was quite unused to inspiring. Obviously the Quabarl family had been woe-fully befooled, but a certain amount of relief came with the knowledge.

'How tiresome for you, dear Carlotta,' said her hostess, when the overdue guest ultimately arrived; 'how very tiresome losing your train and having to stop overnight in a strange place.'

'Oh, dear, no,' said Lady Carlotta; 'not at all tiresome – for me.'

The Elk

Teresa, Mrs Thropplestance, was the richest and most intractable old woman in the county of Woldshire. In her dealings with the world in general her manner suggested a blend between a Mistress of the Robes and a Master of Foxhounds, with the vocabulary of both. In her domestic circle she comported herself in the arbitrary style that one attributes, probably without the least justification, to an American political Boss in the bosom of his caucus. The late Theodore Thropplestance had left her, some thirty-five years ago, in absolute possession of a considerable fortune, a large landed property, and a gallery full of valuable pictures. In those intervening years she had out-lived her son and quarrelled with her elder grandson, who had married without her consent or approval. Bertie Thropplestance, her younger grandson, was the heir-designate to her property, and as such he was a centre of interest and concern to some half-hundred ambitious mothers with daughters of marriageable age. Bertie was an amiable, easy-going young man, who was quite ready to marry any one who was favourably recommended to his notice, but he was not going to waste his time in falling in love with any one who would come under his grandmother's veto. The favourable recommendation would have to come from Mrs Thropplestance.

Teresa's house-parties were always rounded off with a plentiful garnishing of presentable young women and alert, attendant mothers, but the old lady was emphatically discouraging whenever any one of her girl guests became at all likely to outbid the others as a possible granddaughter-in-law. It was the inheritance of her fortune and estate that was in question, and she was evidently disposed to exercise and enjoy her powers of selection and rejection to the utmost. Bertie's preferences did not greatly matter; he was of the sort who can be stolidly happy with any kind of wife; he had cheerfully put up with his grandmother all his life, so he was not likely to fret and fume over anything that might befall him in the way of a helpmate.

The party that gathered under Teresa's roof in Christmas week of the year nineteen-hundred-and-something was of smaller proportions than usual, and Mrs Yonelet, who formed one of the party, was inclined to deduce hopeful augury from this circumstance. Dora Yonelet and Bertie were so obviously made for one another, she confided to the vicar's wife, and if the old lady were accustomed to seeing them about a lot together she might adopt the view that they would make a suitable married couple.

'People soon get used to an idea if it is dangled constantly before their eyes' said Mrs Yonelet hopefully, 'and the more often Teresa sees those young people together, happy in each other's company, the more she will get to take a kindly interest in Dora as a possible and desirable wife for Bertie.'

'My dear,' said the vicar's wife resignedly, 'my own Sybil was thrown together with Bertie under the most romantic circumstances – I'll tell you about it some day – but it made no impression whatever on Teresa; she put her foot down in the most uncompromising fashion, and Sybil married an Indian civilian.'

'Quite right of her,' said Mrs Yonelet with vague approval; 'it's what any girl of spirit would have done. Still, that was a year or two ago, I believe; Bertie is older now, and so is Teresa. Naturally she must be anxious to see him settled.'

The vicar's wife reflected that Teresa seemed to be the one person who showed no immediate anxiety to supply Bertie with a wife, but she kept the thought to herself.

Mrs Yonelet was a woman of resourceful energy and generalship; she involved the other members of the house-party, the deadweight, so to speak, in all manner of exercises and occupations that segregated them from Bertie and Dora, who were left to their own devisings – that is to say, to Dora's devisings and Bertie's accommodating acquiescence. Dora helped in the Christmas decorations of the parish church, and Bertie helped her to help.

Together they fed the swans, till the birds went on a dyspepsia-strike, together they played billiards, together they photographed the village almshouses, and, at a respectful distance, the tame elk that browsed in solitary aloofness in the park. It was 'tame' in the sense that it had long ago discarded the least vestige of fear of the human race; nothing in its record encouraged its human neighbours to feel a reciprocal confidence.

Whatever sport or exercise or occupation Bertie and Dora indulged in together was unfailingly chronicled and advertised by Mrs Yonelet for the due enlightenment of Bertie's grandmother.

'Those two inseparables have just come in from a bicycle ride,' she would announce; 'quite a picture they make, so fresh and glowing after their spin.'

'A picture needing words,' would be Teresa's private comment, and as far as Bertie was concerned she was determined that the words should remain unspoken.

On the afternoon after Christmas Day Mrs Yonelet dashed into the drawing-room, where her hostess was sitting amid a circle of guests and tea-cups and muffin-dishes. Fate had placed what seemed like a trump-card in the hands of the patiently manoeuvring mother. With eyes blazing with excitement and a voice heavily escorted with exclamation marks she made a dramatic announcement.

'Bertie has saved Dora from the elk!'

In swift, excited sentences, broken with maternal emotion, she gave supplementary information as to how the treacherous animal had ambushed Dora as she was hunting for a strayed golf ball, and how Bertie had dashed to her rescue with a stable fork and driven the beast off in the nick of time.

'It was touch and go! She threw her niblick at it, but that didn't stop it. In another moment she would have been crushed beneath its hoofs,' panted Mrs Yonelet.

'The animal is not safe,' said Teresa, handing her agitated guest a cup of tea. 'I forget if you take sugar. I suppose the solitary life it leads has soured its temper. There are muffins in the grate. It's not my fault; I've tried to get it a mate for ever so long. You don't know of any one with a lady elk for sale or exchange, do you?' she asked the company generally.

But Mrs Yonelet was in no humour to listen to talk of elk marriages. The mating of two human beings was the subject uppermost in her mind, and the opportunity for advancing her pet project was too valuable to be neglected.

'Teresa,' she exclaimed impressively, 'after those two young people have been thrown together so dramatically, nothing can be quite the same again between them. Bertie has done more than save Dora's life; he has earned her affection. One cannot help feeling that Fate has consecrated them for one another.'

'Exactly what the vicar's wife said when Bertie saved Sybil from the elk a year or two ago,' observed Teresa placidly; 'I pointed out to her that he had rescued Mirabel

Hicks from the same predicament a few months previously, and that priority really belonged to the gardener's boy, who had been rescued in the January of that year. There is a good deal of sameness in country life, you know.'

'It seems to be a very dangerous animal,' said one of the guests.

'That's what the mother of the gardener's boy said,' remarked Teresa; 'she wanted me to have it destroyed, but I pointed out to her that she had eleven children and I had only one elk. I also gave her a black silk skirt; she said that though there hadn't been a funeral in her family, she felt as if there had been. Anyhow, we parted friends. I can't offer you a silk skirt, Emily, but you may have another cup of tea. As I have already remarked, there are muffins in the grate.'

Teresa closed the discussion, having deftly conveyed the impression that she considered the mother of the gardener's boy had shown a far more reasonable spirit than the parents of other elk-assaulted victims.

'Teresa is devoid of feeling,' said Mrs Yonelet afterwards to the vicar's wife; 'to sit there, talking of muffins, with an appalling tragedy only narrowly averted –'

'Of course you know whom she really intends Bertie to marry?' asked the vicar's wife; 'I've noticed it for some time. The Bickelbys' German governess.'

'A German governess! What an idea!' gasped Mrs Yonelet.

'She's of quite good family, I believe,' said the vicar's wife, 'and not at all the mouse-in-the-background sort of person that governesses are usually supposed to be. In fact, next to Teresa, she's about the most assertive and combative personality in the neighbourhood. She's pointed out to my husband all sorts of errors in his sermons, and she gave Sir Laurence a public lecture on how he ought to handle the hounds. You know how sensitive Sir Laurence is about any criticism of his Mastership, and to have a governess laying down the law to him nearly drove him into a fit. She's behaved like that to every one, except, of course, Teresa, and every one has been defensively rude to her in return. The Bickelbys are simply too afraid of her to get rid of her. Now isn't that exactly the sort of woman whom Teresa would take a delight in installing as her successor? Imagine the discomfort and awkwardness in the county if we suddenly found that she was to be the future hostess at the Hall. Teresa's only regret will be that she won't be alive to see it.'

'But,' objected Mrs Yonelet, 'surely Bertie hasn't shown the least sign of being attracted in that quarter?'

'Oh, she's quite nice-looking in a way, and dresses well, and plays a good game of tennis. She often comes across the park with messages from the Bickelby mansion, and one of these days Bertie will rescue her from the elk, which has become almost a habit with him, and Teresa will say that Fate has consecrated them to one another. Bertie might not be disposed to pay much attention to the consecrations of Fate, but he would not dream of opposing his grandmother.'

The vicar's wife spoke with the quiet authority of one who has intuitive knowledge, and in her heart of hearts Mrs Yonelet believed her.

Six months later the elk had to be destroyed. In a fit of exceptional moroseness it had killed the Bickelbys' German governess. It was an irony of its fate that it should achieve popularity in the last moments of its career; at any rate, it established the record of being the only living thing that had permanently thwarted Teresa Thropplestance's plans.

Dora Yonelet broke off her engagement with an Indian civilian, and married Bertie three months after his grandmother's death – Teresa did not long survive the German governess fiasco. At Christmas time every year young Mrs Thropplestance hangs an extra large festoon of evergreens on the elk horns that decorate the hall.

'It was a fearsome beast,' she observes to Bertie, 'but I always feel that it was instrumental in bringing us together.'

Which, of course, was true.

The Lumber-Room

The children were to be driven, as a special treat, to the sands at Jagborough. Nicholas was not to be of the party; he was in disgrace. Only that morning he had refused to eat his wholesome bread-and-milk on the seemingly frivolous ground that there was a frog in it. Older and wiser and better people had told him that there could not possibly be a frog in his bread-and-milk and that he was not to talk nonsense; he continued, nevertheless, to talk what seemed the veriest nonsense, and described with much detail the colouration and markings of the alleged frog. The dramatic part of the incident was that there really was a frog in Nicholas' basin of bread-and-milk; he had put it there himself, so he felt entitled to know something about it. The sin of taking a frog from the garden and putting it into a bowl of wholesome bread-and-milk was enlarged on at great length, but the fact that stood out clearest in the whole affair, as it presented itself to the mind of Nicholas, was that the older, wiser and better people had been proved to be profoundly in error in

matters about which they had expressed the utmost
assurance.

'You said there couldn't possibly be a frog in my bread-
and-milk; there *was* a frog in my bread-and-milk,' he
repeated, with the insistence of a skilled tactician who
does not intend to shift from favourable ground.

So his boy-cousin and girl-cousin and his quite uninteresting younger brother were to be taken to Jagborough
sands that afternoon and he was to stay at home. His
cousins' aunt, who insisted, by an unwarranted stretch of
imagination, in styling herself his aunt also, had hastily
invented the Jagborough expedition in order to impress
on Nicholas the delights that he had justly forfeited by
his disgraceful conduct at the breakfast-table. It was her
habit, whenever one of the children fell from grace, to
improvise something of a festival nature from which the
offender would be rigorously debarred; if all the children
sinned collectively they were suddenly informed of a circus in a neighbouring town, a circus of unrivalled merit
and uncounted elephants, to which, but for their deprav-
ity, they would have been taken that very day.

A few decent tears were looked for on the part of Nicholas when the moment for the departure of the expedition
arrived. As a matter of fact, however, all the crying was
done by his girl-cousin, who scraped her knee rather
painfully against the step of the carriage as she was scrambling in.

'How she did howl,' said Nicholas cheerfully, as the

party drove off without any of the elation of high spirits that should have characterized it.

'She'll soon get over that,' said the *soi-disant* aunt; 'it will be a glorious afternoon for racing about over those beautiful sands. How they will enjoy themselves!'

'Bobby won't enjoy himself much, and he won't race much either,' said Nicholas with a grim chuckle; 'his boots are hurting him. They're too tight.'

'Why didn't he tell me they were hurting?' asked the aunt with some asperity.

'He told you twice, but you weren't listening. You often don't listen when we tell you important things.'

'You are not to go into the gooseberry garden,' said the aunt, changing the subject.

'Why not?' demanded Nicholas.

'Because you are in disgrace,' said the aunt loftily.

Nicholas did not admit the flawlessness of the reasoning; he felt perfectly capable of being in disgrace and in a gooseberry garden at the same moment. His face took on an expression of considerable obstinacy. It was clear to his aunt that he was determined to get into the gooseberry garden, 'only,' as she remarked to herself, 'because I have told him he is not to.'

Now the gooseberry garden had two doors by which it might be entered, and once a small person like Nicholas could slip in there he could effectually disappear from view amid the masking growth of artichokes, raspberry canes, and fruit bushes. The aunt had many other things to do that afternoon, but she spent an hour or two in trivial gardening operations among flower beds and shrubberies, whence she could keep a watchful eye on the two doors that led to the forbidden paradise. She was a woman of few ideas, with immense powers of concentration.

Nicholas made one or two sorties into the front garden, wriggling his way with obvious stealth of purpose towards one or other of the doors, but never able for a moment to evade the aunt's watchful eye. As a matter of fact, he had no intention of trying to get into the gooseberry garden, but it was extremely convenient for him that his aunt should believe that he had; it was a belief that would keep her on self-imposed sentry-duty for the greater part of the afternoon. Having thoroughly confirmed and fortified her suspicions, Nicholas slipped back into the house and rapidly put into execution a plan of action that had long germinated in his brain. By standing on a chair in the library one could reach a shelf on which reposed a fat, important-looking key. The key was as important as it looked; it was the instrument which kept the mysteries of the lumber-room secure from unauthorized intrusion, which opened a way only for aunts and such-like privileged persons. Nicholas had not much experience of the art of fitting keys into keyholes and turning locks, but for some days past he had practised with the key of the school-room door; he did not believe in trusting too much to luck and accident. The key turned stiffly in the lock, but it turned. The door opened, and Nicholas was in an unknown land, compared with which the gooseberry garden was a stale delight, a mere material pleasure.

Often and often Nicholas had pictured to himself what the lumber-room might be like, that region that was so carefully sealed from youthful eyes and concerning which no questions were ever answered. It came up to his expectations. In the first place it was large and dimly lit, one high window opening on to the forbidden garden being its only source of illumination. In the second place it was a storehouse of unimagined treasures. The aunt-by-assertion was one of those people who think that things spoil by use and consign them to dust and damp by way of preserving them. Such parts of the house as Nicholas knew best were rather bare and cheerless, but here there were wonderful things for the eye to feast on. First and foremost there was a piece of framed tapestry that was evidently meant to be a fire-screen. To Nicholas it was a living, breathing story; he sat down on a roll of Indian hangings, glowing in wonderful colours beneath a layer of dust, and took in all the details of the tapestry picture. A man, dressed in the hunting costume of some remote period, had just transfixed a stag with an arrow; it could not have been a difficult shot because the stag was only one or two paces away from him; in the thickly growing vegetation that the picture suggested it would not have been difficult to creep up to a feeding stag, and the two spotted dogs that were springing forward to join in the chase had evidently been trained to keep to heel till the arrow was discharged. That part of the picture was simple, if interesting, but did the huntsman see, what Nicholas saw, that four galloping wolves were coming in his direction through the wood? There might be more than four of them hidden behind the trees, and in any case would the man and his dogs be able to cope with the four wolves if they made an attack? The man had only two arrows left in his quiver, and he might miss with one or both of them; all one knew about his skill in shooting was that he could hit a large stag at a ridiculously short range. Nicholas sat for many golden minutes revolving the possibilities of the scene; he was inclined to think that there were more than four wolves and that the man and his dogs were in a tight corner.

But there were other objects of delight and interest claiming his instant attention: here were quaint twisted candlesticks in the shape of snakes, and a teapot fashioned like a china duck, out of whose open beak the tea was supposed to come. How dull and shapeless the nursery teapot seemed in comparison! And there was a carved sandalwood box packed tight with aromatic cotton-wool, and between the layers of cotton-wool were little brass figures, hump-necked bulls, and peacocks and goblins, delightful to see and to handle. Less promising in appearance was a large square book with plain black covers; Nicholas peeped into it, and, behold, it was full of coloured pictures of birds. And such birds! In the garden, and in the lanes when he went for a walk, Nicholas came across a few birds, of which the largest were an occasional magpie or wood-pigeon; here were herons and bustards, kites, toucans, tiger-bitterns, brush turkeys, ibises, golden pheasants, a whole portrait gallery of undreamed-of creatures. And as he was admiring the colouring of the mandarin duck and assigning a life-history to it, the voice of his aunt in shrill vociferation of his name came from the gooseberry garden without. She had grown suspicious at his long disappearance, and had leapt to the conclusion that he had climbed over the wall behind the sheltering screen of the lilac bushes; she was now engaged in energetic and rather hopeless search for him among the artichokes and raspberry canes.

'Nicholas, Nicholas!' she screamed, 'you are to come out of this at once. It's no use trying to hide there; I can see you all the time.'

It was probably the first time for twenty years that any one had smiled in that lumber-room.

Presently the angry repetitions of Nicholas' name gave way to a shriek, and a cry for somebody to come quickly. Nicholas shut the book, restored it carefully to its place in a corner, and shook some dust from a neighbouring pile of newspapers over it. Then he crept from the room, locked the door, and replaced the key exactly where he had found it. His aunt was still calling his name when he sauntered into the front garden.

'Who's calling?' he asked.

'Me,' came the answer from the other side of the wall; 'didn't you hear me? I've been looking for you in the gooseberry garden, and I've slipped into the rain-water tank. Luckily there's no water in it, but the sides are slippery and I can't get out. Fetch the little ladder from under the cherry tree –'

'I was told I wasn't to go into the gooseberry garden,' said Nicholas promptly.

'I told you not to, and now I tell you that you may,' came the voice from the rain-water tank, rather impatiently.

'Your voice doesn't sound like aunt's,' objected Nicholas; 'you may be the Evil One tempting me to be disobedient. Aunt often tells me that the Evil One tempts me and that I always yield. This time I'm not going to yield.'

'Don't talk nonsense,' said the prisoner in the tank; 'go and fetch the ladder.'

'Will there be strawberry jam for tea?' asked Nicholas innocently.

'Certainly there will be,' said the aunt, privately resolving that Nicholas should have none of it.

'Now I know that you are the Evil One and not aunt,' shouted Nicholas gleefully; 'when we asked aunt for strawberry jam yesterday she said there wasn't any. I know there are four jars of it in the store cupboard, because I looked, and of course you know it's there, but *she* doesn't, because she said there wasn't any. Oh, Devil, you *have* sold yourself!'

There was an unusual sense of luxury in being able to talk to an aunt as though one was talking to the Evil One, but Nicholas knew, with childish discernment, that such luxuries were not to be overindulged in. He walked noisily away, and it was a kitchenmaid, in search of parsley, who eventually rescued the aunt from the rain-water tank.

Tea that evening was partaken of in a fearsome silence. The tide had been at its highest when the children had arrived at Jagborough Cove, so there had been no sands to play on – a circumstance that the aunt had overlooked in the haste of organizing her punitive expedition. The tightness of Bobby's boots had had disastrous effect on his temper the whole of the afternoon, and altogether the children could not have been said to have enjoyed themselves. The aunt maintained the frozen muteness of one who has suffered undignified and unmerited detention in a rain-water tank for thirty-five minutes. As for Nicholas, he, too, was silent, in the absorption of one who has much to think about; it was just possible, he considered, that the huntsman would escape with his hounds while the wolves feasted on the stricken stag.

The Interlopers

In a forest of mixed growth somewhere on the eastern spurs of the Carpathians, a man stood one winter night watching and listening, as though he waited for some beast of the woods to come within the range of his vision, and, later, of his rifle. But the game for whose presence he kept so keen an outlook was none that figured in the sportsman's calendar as lawful and proper for the chase; Ulrich von Gradwitz patrolled the dark forest in quest of a human enemy.

The forest lands of Gradwitz were of wide extent and well stocked with game; the narrow strip of precipitous woodland that lay on its outskirt was not remarkable for the game it harboured or the shooting it afforded, but it was the most jealously guarded of all its owner's territorial possessions. A famous lawsuit, in the days of his grandfather, had wrested it from the illegal possession of a neighbouring family of petty landowners; the dispossessed party had never acquiesced in the judgment of the Courts, and a long series of poaching affrays and similar scandals had embittered the relationships between the families for three generations. The neighbour feud had grown into a personal one since Ulrich had come to be head of his family; if there was a man in the world whom he detested and wished ill to it was Georg Znaeym, the inheritor of the quarrel and the tireless game-snatcher and raider of the disputed border-forest. The feud might, perhaps, have died down or been compromised if the personal ill-will of the two men had not stood in the way; as boys they had thirsted for one another's blood, as men each prayed that misfortune might fall on the other, and this wind-scourged winter night Ulrich had banded together his foresters to watch the dark forest, not in quest of four-footed quarry, but to keep a look-out for the prowling thieves whom he suspected of being afoot from across the land boundary. The roebuck, which usually kept in the sheltered hollows during a storm-wind, were running like driven things tonight, and there was movement and unrest among the creatures that were wont to sleep through the dark hours. Assuredly there was a disturbing element in the forest, and Ulrich could guess the quarter from whence it came.

He strayed away by himself from the watchers whom he had placed in ambush on the crest of the hill, and wandered far down the steep slopes amid the wild tangle of undergrowth, peering through the tree-trunks and listening through the whistling and skirling of the wind and the restless beating of the branches for sight or sound of the marauders. If only on this wild night, in this dark, lone spot, he might come across Georg Znaeym, man to man, with none to witness – that was the wish that was uppermost in his thoughts. And as he stepped round the trunk of a huge beech he came face to face with the man he sought.

The two enemies stood glaring at one another for a long silent moment. Each had a rifle in his hand, each had hate in his heart and murder uppermost in his mind. The chance had come to give full play to the passions of a lifetime. But a man who has been brought up under the code of a restraining civilization cannot easily nerve himself to shoot down his neighbour in cold blood and without word spoken, except for an offence against his hearth and honour. And before the moment of hesitation had given way to action a deed of Nature's own violence overwhelmed them both. A fierce shriek of the storm had been answered by a splitting crash over their heads, and ere they could leap aside a mass of falling beech tree had thundered down on them. Ulrich von Gradwitz found himself stretched on the ground, one arm numb beneath him and the other held almost as helplessly in a tight tangle of forked branches, while both legs were pinned beneath the fallen mass. His heavy shooting-boots had saved his feet from being crushed to pieces, but if his fractures were not as serious as they might have been, at least it was evident that he could not move from his present position till some one came to release him.

The descending twigs had slashed the skin of his face, and he had to wink away some drops of blood from his eyelashes before he could take in a general view of the disaster. At his side, so near that under ordinary circumstances he could almost have touched him, lay Georg Znaeym, alive and struggling, but obviously as helplessly pinioned down as himself. All round them lay a thick-strewn wreckage of splintered branches and broken twigs.

Relief at being alive and exasperation at his captive plight brought a strange medley of pious thank-offerings and sharp curses to Ulrich's lips. Georg, who was nearly blinded with the blood which trickled across his eyes, stopped his struggling for a moment to listen, and then gave a short, snarling laugh.

'So you're not killed, as you ought to be, but you're caught, anyway,' he cried; 'caught fast. Ho, what a jest, Ulrich von Gradwitz snared in his stolen forest. There's real justice for you!'

And he laughed again, mockingly and savagely.

'I'm caught in my own forest-land,' retorted Ulrich. 'When my men come to release us you will wish, perhaps, that you were in a better plight than caught poaching on a neighbour's land, shame on you.'

Georg was silent for a moment; then he answered quietly:

'Are you sure that your men will find much to release? I have men, too, in the forest tonight, close behind me, and *they* will be here first and do the releasing. When they drag me out from under these damned branches it won't need much clumsiness on their part to roll this mass of trunk right over on the top of you. Your men will find you dead under a fallen beech tree. For form's sake I shall send my condolences to your family.'

'It is a useful hint,' said Ulrich fiercely. 'My men had orders to follow in ten minutes' time, seven of which must have gone by already, and when they get me out – I will remember the hint. Only as you will have met your death poaching on my lands I don't think I can decently send any message of condolence to your family.'

'Good,' snarled Georg, 'good. We fight this quarrel out to the death, you and I and our foresters, with no cursed interlopers to come between us. Death and damnation to you, Ulrich von Gradwitz.'

'The same to you, Georg Znaeym, forest-thief, game-snatcher.'

Both men spoke with the bitterness of possible defeat before them, for each knew that it might be long before his men would seek him out or find him; it was a bare matter of chance which party would arrive first on the scene.

Both had now given up the useless struggle to free themselves from the mass of wood that held them down; Ulrich limited his endeavours to an effort to bring his one partially free arm near enough to his outer coat-pocket to draw out his wine-flask. Even when he had accomplished that operation it was long before he could manage the unscrewing of the stopper or get any of the liquid down his throat. But what a Heaven-sent draught it seemed! It was an open winter, and little snow had fallen as yet, hence the captives suffered less from the cold than might have been the case at that season of the year; nevertheless, the wine was warming and reviving to the wounded man, and he looked across with something like a throb of pity to where his enemy lay, just keeping the groans of pain and weariness from crossing his lips.

'Could you reach this flask if I threw it over to you?' asked Ulrich suddenly; 'there is good wine in it, and one may as well be as comfortable as one can. Let us drink, even if tonight one of us dies.'

'No, I can scarcely see anything; there is so much blood caked round my eyes,' said Georg, 'and in any case I don't drink wine with an enemy.'

Ulrich was silent for a few minutes, and lay listening to the weary screeching of the wind. An idea was slowly forming and growing in his brain, an idea that gained strength every time that he looked across at the man who was fighting so grimly against pain and exhaustion. In the pain and languor that Ulrich himself was feeling the old fierce hatred seemed to be dying down.

'Neighbour,' he said presently, 'do as you please if your men come first. It was a fair compact. But as for me, I've changed my mind. If my men are the first to come you shall be the first to be helped, as though you were my guest. We have quarrelled like devils all our lives over this stupid strip of forest, where the trees can't even stand upright in a breath of wind. Lying here tonight, thinking, I've come to think we've been rather fools; there are better things in life than getting the better of a boundary dispute. Neighbour, if you will help me to bury the old quarrel I – I will ask you to be my friend.'

Georg Znaeym was silent for so long that Ulrich thought, perhaps, he had fainted with the pain of his injuries. Then he spoke slowly and in jerks.

'How the whole region would stare and gabble if we rode into the market-square together. No one living can remember seeing a Znaeym and a von Gradwitz talking to one another in friendship. And what peace there would be among the forester folk if we ended our feud tonight. And if we choose to make peace among our people there is none other to interfere, no interlopers from outside . . . You would come and keep the Sylvester night beneath my roof, and I would come and feast on some high day at your castle . . . I would never fire a shot on your land, save when you invited me as a guest; and you should come and shoot with me down in the marshes where the wildfowl are. In all the countryside there are none that could hinder if we willed to make peace. I never thought to have wanted to do other than hate you all my life, but I think I have changed my mind about things too, this last half-hour. And you offered me your wine-flask . . . Ulrich von Gradwitz, I will be your friend.'

For a space both men were silent, turning over in their minds the wonderful changes that this dramatic reconciliation would bring about. In the cold, gloomy forest, with the wind tearing in fitful gusts through the naked branches and whistling round the tree-trunks, they lay and waited for the help that would now bring release and succour to both parties. And each prayed a private prayer that his men might be the first to arrive, so that he might be the first to show honourable attention to the enemy that had become a friend.

Presently, as the wind dropped for a moment, Ulrich broke silence.

'Let's shout for help,' he said; 'in this lull our voices may carry a little way.'

'They won't carry far through the trees and under-growth,' said Georg, 'but we can try. Together, then.'

The two raised their voices in a prolonged hunting call.

'Together again,' said Ulrich a few minutes later, after listening in vain for an answering halloo.

'I heard something that time, I think,' said Ulrich.

'I heard nothing but the pestilential wind,' said Georg hoarsely.

There was silence again for some minutes, and then Ulrich gave a joyful cry.

'I can see figures coming through the wood. They are following in the way I came down the hillside.'

Both men raised their voices in as loud a shout as they could muster.

'They hear us! They've stopped. Now they see us. They're running down the hill towards us,' cried Ulrich.

'How many of them are there?' asked Georg.

'I can't see distinctly,' said Ulrich; 'nine or ten.'

'Then they are yours,' said Georg; 'I had only seven out with me.'

'They are making all the speed they can, brave lads,' said Ulrich gladly.

'Are they your men?' asked Georg. 'Are they your men?' he repeated impatiently as Ulrich did not answer.

'No,' said Ulrich with a laugh, the idiotic chattering laugh of a man unstrung with hideous fear.

'Who are they?' asked Georg quickly, straining his eyes to see what the other would gladly not have seen.

'*Wolves.*'

Bertie's Christmas Eve

It was Christmas Eve, and the family circle of Luke Steffink, Esq., was aglow with the amiability and random mirth which the occasion demanded. A long and lavish dinner had been partaken of, waits had been round and sung carols, the house-party had regaled itself with more carolling on its own account, and there had been romping which, even in a pulpit reference, could not have been condemned as ragging. In the midst of the general glow, however, there was one black unkindled cinder.

Bertie Steffink, nephew of the aforementioned Luke, had early in life adopted the profession of ne'er-do-weel; his father had been something of the kind before him. At the age of eighteen Bertie had commenced that round of visits to our Colonial possessions, so seemly and desirable in the case of a Prince of the Blood, so suggestive of insincerity in a young man of the middle-class. He had gone to grow tea in Ceylon and fruit in British Columbia, and to help sheep to grow wool in Australia. At the age of twenty he had just returned from some similar errand in Canada, from which it may be gathered that the trial he gave to these various experiments was of the summary drum-head nature. Luke Steffink, who fulfilled the troubled rôle of guardian and deputy-parent to Bertie, deplored the persistent manifestation of the homing instinct on his nephew's part, and his solemn thanks earlier in the day for the blessing of reporting a united family had no reference to Bertie's return.

Arrangements had been promptly made for packing the youth off to a distant corner of Rhodesia, whence return would be a difficult matter; the journey to this uninviting destination was imminent, in fact a more careful and willing traveller would have already begun to think about his packing. Hence Bertie was in no mood to share in the festive spirit which displayed itself around him, and resentment smouldered within him at the eager, self-absorbed discussion of social plans for the coming months which he heard on all sides. Beyond depressing his uncle and the family circle generally by singing 'Say au revoir, and not good-bye,' he had taken no part in the evening's conviviality.

Eleven o'clock had struck some half-hour ago, and the elder Steffinks began to throw out suggestions leading up to that process which they called retiring for the night.

'Come, Teddie, it's time you were in your little bed, you know,' said Luke Steffink to his thirteen-year-old son.

'That's where we all ought to be,' said Mrs Steffink.

'There wouldn't be room,' said Bertie.

The remark was considered to border on the scandalous; everybody ate raisins and almonds with the nervous industry of sheep feeding during threatening weather.

'In Russia,' said Horace Bordenby, who was staying in the house as a Christmas guest, 'I've read that the peasants believe that if you go into a cow-house or stable at midnight on Christmas Eve you will hear the animals talk. They're supposed to have the gift of speech at that one moment of the year.'

'Oh, *do* let's *all* go down to the cow-house and listen to what they've got to say?' exclaimed Beryl, to whom anything was thrilling and amusing if you did it in a troop.

Mrs Steffink made a laughing protest, but gave a virtual consent by saying, 'We must all wrap up well, then.' The idea seemed a scatterbrained one to her, and almost heathenish, but it afforded an opportunity for 'throwing the young people together,' and as such she welcomed it. Mr Horace Bordenby was a young man with quite substantial prospects, and he had danced with Beryl at a local subscription ball a sufficient number of times to warrant the authorized inquiry on the part of the neighbours whether 'there was anything in it.' Though Mrs Steffink would not have put it in so many words, she shared the idea of the Russian peasantry that on this night the beast might speak.

The cow-house stood at the junction of the garden with a small paddock, an isolated survival, in a suburban neighbourhood, of what had once been a small farm. Luke Steffink was complacently proud of his cow-house and his two cows; he felt that they gave him a stamp of solidity which no number of Wyandottes or Orpingtons could impart. They even seemed to link him in a sort of inconsequent way with those patriarchs who derived importance from their floating capital of flocks and herds, he-asses and she-asses. It had been an anxious and momentous occasion when he had had to decide definitely between 'the Byre' and 'the Ranch' for the naming of his villa residence. A December midnight was hardly the moment he would have chosen for showing his farm-building to visitors, but since it was a fine night, and the young people were anxious for an excuse for a mild frolic, Luke consented to chaperon the expedition. The servants had long since gone to bed, so the house was left in charge of Bertie, who scornfully declined to stir out on the pretext of listening to bovine conversation.

'We must go quietly,' said Luke, as he headed the procession of giggling young folk, brought up in the rear by the shawled and hooded figure of Mrs Steffink; 'I've always laid stress on keeping this a quiet and orderly neighbourhood.'

It was a few minutes to midnight when the party reached the cow-house and made its way in by the light of Luke's stable lantern. For a moment every one stood in silence, almost with a feeling of being in church.

'Daisy – the one lying down – is by a shorthorn bull

out of a Guernsey cow,' announced Luke in a hushed voice, which was in keeping with the foregoing impression.

'Is she?' said Bordenby, rather as if he had expected her to be by Rembrandt.

'Myrtle is –'

Myrtle's family history was cut short by a little scream from the women of the party.

The cow-house door had closed noiselessly behind them and the key had turned gratingly in the lock; then they heard Bertie's voice pleasantly wishing them good night and his footsteps retreating along the garden path.

Luke Steffink strode to the window; it was a small square opening of the old-fashioned sort, with iron bars let into the stonework.

'Unlock the door this instant,' he shouted, with as much air of menacing authority as a hen might assume when screaming through the bars of a coop at a marauding hawk. In reply to his summons the hall-door closed with a defiant bang.

A neighbouring clock struck the hour of midnight. If the cows had received the gift of human speech at that moment they would not have been able to make themselves heard. Seven or eight other voices were engaged in describing Bertie's present conduct and his general character at a high pressure of excitement and indignation.

In the course of half an hour or so everything that it was permissible to say about Bertie had been said some dozens of times, and other topics began to come to the

front – the extreme mustiness of the cow-house, the possibility of it catching fire, and the probability of it being
a Rowton House for the vagrant rats of the neighbourhood. And still no sign of deliverance came to the
unwilling vigil-keepers.

Towards one o'clock the sound of rather boisterous
and undisciplined carol-singing approached rapidly, and
came to a sudden anchorage, apparently just outside the
garden-gate. A motor-load of youthful 'bloods,' in a high
state of conviviality, had made a temporary halt for
repairs; the stoppage, however, did not extend to the
vocal efforts of the party, and the watchers in the cow-
shed were treated to a highly unauthorized rendering of
'Good King Wenceslas,' in which the adjective 'good'
appeared to be very carelessly applied.

The noise had the effect of bringing Bertie out into
the garden, but he utterly ignored the pale, angry faces
peering out at the cow-house window, and concentrated
his attention on the revellers outside the gate.

'Wassail, you chaps!' he shouted.

'Wassail, old sport!' they shouted back; 'we'd jolly well
drink y'r health, only we've nothing to drink it in.'

'Come and wassail inside,' said Bertie hospitably; 'I'm
all alone, and there's heaps of "wet."'

They were total strangers, but his touch of kindness
made them instantly his kin. In another moment the
unauthorized version of King Wenceslas, which, like many
other scandals, grew worse on repetition, went echoing

up the garden path; two of the revellers gave an impromptu performance on the way by executing the staircase waltz up the terraces of what Luke Steffink, hitherto with some justification, called his rock-garden. The rock part of it was still there when the waltz had been accorded its third encore. Luke, more than ever like a cooped hen behind the cow-house bars, was in a position to realize the feelings of concert-goers unable to countermand the call for an encore which they neither desire nor deserve.

The hall door closed with a bang on Bertie's guests, and the sounds of merriment became faint and muffled to the weary watchers at the other end of the garden. Presently two ominous pops, in quick succession, made themselves distinctly heard.

'They've got at the champagne!' exclaimed Mrs Steffink.

'Perhaps it's the sparkling Moselle,' said Luke hopefully.

Three or four more pops were heard.

'The champagne *and* the sparkling Moselle,' said Mrs Steffink.

Luke uncorked an expletive which, like brandy in a temperance household, was only used on rare emergencies. Mr Horace Bordenby had been making use of similar expressions under his breath for a considerable time past. The experiment of 'throwing the young people together' had been prolonged beyond a point when it was likely to produce any romantic result.

Some forty minutes later the hall door opened and disgorged a crowd that had thrown off any restraint of shyness that might have influenced its earlier actions. Its vocal efforts in the direction of carol-singing were now supplemented by instrumental music; a Christmas-tree that had been prepared for the children of the gardener and other household retainers had yielded a rich spoil of tin trumpets, rattles, and drums. The life-story of King Wenceslas had been dropped, Luke was thankful to notice, but it was intensely irritating for the chilled prisoners in the cow-house to be told that it was 'a hot time in the old town tonight,' together with some accurate but entirely superfluous information as to the imminence of Christmas morning. Judging by the protests which began to be shouted from the upper windows of neighbouring houses, the sentiments prevailing in the cow-house were heartily echoed in other quarters.

The revellers found their car, and, what was more remarkable, managed to drive off in it, with a parting fanfare of tin trumpets. The lively beat of a drum disclosed the fact that the master of the revels remained on the scene.

'Bertie!' came in an angry, imploring chorus of shouts and screams from the cow-house window.

'Hullo,' cried the owner of the name, turning his rather errant steps in the direction of the summons; 'are you people still there? Must have heard everything cows got to say by this time. If you haven't, no use waiting. After all, it's a Russian legend, and Russian Chrismush Eve not due for 'nother fortnight. Better come out.'

After one or two ineffectual attempts he managed to pitch the key of the cow-house door in through the window. Then, lifting his voice in the strains of 'I'm afraid to go home in the dark,' with a lusty drum accompaniment, he led the way back to the house. The hurried procession of the released that followed in his steps came in for a good deal of the adverse comment that his exuberant display had evoked.

It was the happiest Christmas Eve he had ever spent. To quote his own words, he had a rotten Christmas.